The Wise Child & Magic

The Wise Child & Magic

Three Plays

Christopher Vened

COPYRIGHT INFORMATION

Manufactured in the United States of America

The Library of Congress Publication Data:

Vened, Christoper (pseudonym of Krzysztof "Christopher" Szwaja)
    [Plays. English.]. The Wise Child and Magic. Three Plays.
Christopher Vened, author.

124 pages (x pp. prefatory matter, and 114 pp. text); 6 in x 9 in. Written in English.

ISBN 978-1-945938-75-7 paperback
ISBN 978-1-945938-37-5 hardcover
ISBN 978-1-945938-76-4 eBook in ePUB format

I. Vened, Christopher -Theatrical Plays. II. Title.

10 9 8 7 6 5 4 3 2 1

For Rebecca, my wife

~ The Wise Child & Magic ~

Three Plays

by

Christopher Vened

adapted from

The Emperor's New Clothes
by Hans Christian Andersen

The Maiden without Hands
from Grimms' Fairy Tales

and *Psyche*
by Hans Christian Andersen

~ Table of Contents ~

~ Introduction ~

The Wise Child and Magic: Three Plays contains three one-act plays that are adapted from classical fairy tales.

The Emperor's New Clothes, originally written by Hans Christian Andersen, is a satire on human vanity, narcissism, mendacity, and pretentiousness. Everybody sees that the emperor is naked but only an innocent child dares to speak about it. Why is only this child truthful to himself but all the adults embrace falsehood? Well, they are all afraid to be canceled, but the child does not know how to lie yet. The play is absurdly funny, but it also has a bitter message for contemporary times about the possible dangers and falsehood of political correctness. Let it be a warning that people must be free to speak the truth. The play is set up in rococo style, and it shall be highly theatrical in realization.

The Maiden Without Hands, originally written by an anonymous writer, is included in *Grimms' Fairy Tales*. It is a surreal story about the fears and hopes a girl experiences during puberty. At times the story is like a nightmare, at others, like a beautiful dream. Nothing is realistic about it, but everything is true. The story explores the depth of her psyche through symbolic images, and its function is to initiate adolescent girls to adulthood. The play is set up in the Early Medieval Period that is full of fantastic creatures, superstition, and miracles. It has the feel of a poetical folk fairy tale.

Psyche is based on Hans Christian Andersen's lesser-known story of the same title. As of yet, it has never been adapted to anything else, which is curious because it is one of his best works. It is not a fairy tale, as most of his works are, but a realistic story.

Still, it features the supernatural that occurs in art. It is a tragic story about a talented Renaissance artist who seeks perfection in art. But he gives up his vocation as a sculptor because a girl breaks his heart, and then he spends the rest of his life in a monastery. He escapes from life because it is too dirty for him, and he can't handle it. He hides in the monastery to find a heavenly peace but instead he is tormented by the devil from within. The moral of the story is this: follow your calling and don't waste your talent because you will suffer.

~ Acknowledgment ~

The cover image of a mysterious wooden structure is my photo of the Spirit of the Mountains (Duch Gór) cottage that comes from the Garden of Fairytales (Ogród Bajek), in Międzygórze, Poland, a mountain resort, where I grew up. There is a story about it, or, rather, many stories and it is personal to me, because my family was running the site. It was an enchanting place and quite unusual, originally built (without using mechanical tools) by a German man, Izydor Kriesten, only from what he found in the forest: bark, branches, roots, and stones. I spent many days in this garden during my early childhood because my Grandma was a guide for tourists there. She was telling them the fairy tales that those artifacts illustrated. I loved my Grandma's stories and they became my inspiration. I'm especially thankful for all the incredible support of my wife, Rebecca Robertson-Szwaja, especially her patience, continuing encouragement and editorial skills. I feel lucky to have Maja Trochimczyk as my publisher. I would like to thank her for her creative input. She designed the cover and came up with the tile of the book.

~ Christopher Vened

~ The Emperor's New Clothes ~

~ A Play ~

by

Christopher Vened

Based on

Hans Christian Andersen's Fairy Tale
of the Same Title

~ CAST OF CHARACTERS ~

The Narrator: A storyteller who is also a master of ceremony

The Emperor: He loves to dress in beautiful new clothes

Weaver One: A swindler who pretends to be a weaver

Weaver Two: A swindler who pretends to be a weaver

Prime Minister: A good-natured old man on the surface, but unscrupulous underneath

The Emperor's Councilor: A cunning and calculated man

The Emperor's Courtiers: Two/Four ostentatious flatterers

The Emperor's Dresser One: A court master tailor

The Emperor's Dresser Two: A court master tailor

The Emperor's Servants: Four train and canopy carriers

The Master of Ceremony: He directs the parade

A Little Child: He is innocent and honest

The Father: He listens to his son

The Town Folk: All the available actors

~ SCENES ~

The Emperor's Clothes Closet

The Emperor's Council Chamber

The Weavers' Workshop

The Town Street

~ TIME ~

The Early 18th Century (Rococo)

SET UP: An Empty Stage

THE NARRATOR speaks directly to the audience.

THE NARRATOR: Many, many years ago there was an emperor who loved to wear beautiful clothes and spent a lot of time trying them on in front of the mirror.

~ SCENE 1 ~

SET UP: The Emperor's Clothes' Closet

THE EMPEROR tries on clothes in front of an imaginary mirror. TWO DRESSERS assist him. COURTIERS admire and flatter him.

THE EMPEROR: How does it fit?

COURTIER ONE: Perfectly well, Your Majesty.

THE EMPEROR: How do I look?

COURTIER TWO: You look splendid, Your Highness.

The Emperor regards himself in the mirror.

THE EMPEROR: Indeed.

The Emperor kisses the imaginary mirror.

THE EMPEROR: I love it!

The Emperor parades himself in front of the mirror; his Courtiers' admiration and flattery become theatrical.

COURTIER THREE: You look magnificent, Your Majesty!

COURTIER FOUR: Admirable.

The Narrator steps in and with one magical gesture makes everybody freeze into a tableau.

THE NARRATOR: Look at that: this is a tableau of vanity: an emperor dressing himself in new clothes and admiring himself in the mirror for hours. He is only in love with himself, like Narcissus. The Emperor is supposed to be with his ministers in his council chamber, not with his dressers in his clothes closet. But he does not care about his soldiers, or attending the theater, or even going for a drive in the park, unless it is to show off his new clothes. He has an outfit for every hour of the day. And he spends all his money on his new attire. Vanity is a vice that can ruin the country! And it must not go on endlessly unpunished. There are consequences to all of our actions, even the most trivial ones. Look what happens next:

The Narrator gestures toward the wings, and two swindlers, who pretend to be WEAVERS, enter the stage.

THE NARRATOR: One day two swindlers came to town and pretended to be weavers.

WEAVERS, *shouting on the street in unison*: We can make the most extraordinary cloth in the world.

THE NARRATOR: When The Emperor heard that rumor, he became intrigued and invited them to the palace.

The tableau unfreezes; The Emperor sits on the throne surrounded by the court; the Weavers enter the chamber.

MASTER OF CEREMONY: Your Majesty, the Weavers who recently came to town are waiting for your reception.

THE EMPEROR: Bring them in.

MASTER OF CEREMONY: Come forth, Weavers, and bow to The Emperor.

The Weavers come forth and bow.

WEAVERS: Your Majesty, your humble subjects.

THE EMPEROR: Humble?

WEAVER ONE: Yes, Your Highness.

THE EMPEROR, *making fun of the Weavers:* Nothing bores me more than humble people.

The Courtiers laugh at The Emperor's joke.

WEAVER TWO: We are also proud weavers, Your Highness.

THE EMPEROR: What could you weave for me?

WEAVER ONE: We could weave for you the most beautiful cloth in the world.

THE EMPEROR: All weavers say that.

WEAVER TWO: Your Majesty, nothing compares to our cloth: its colors and the patterns are not only the most beautiful, but also the cloth has the strange quality of being invisible to anyone who is unfit for his office or unforgivably stupid.

THE EMPEROR: This is truly marvelous. Now if I had robes cut from that material, I would know which of my councilors was unfit for his office, ha, ha, ha, and I would be able to pick which of my subjects were more clever than myself, ha, ha, ha.... You must weave some material for me!

WEAVERS: We will, Your Majesty.

THE EMPEROR: When can you start?

WEAVERS: As soon as we set up our workshop in town.

THE EMPEROR: Oh, don't bother. We will arrange a workshop for you in the palace, and you will start working at once. Isn't it a splendid idea, Prime Minister?

PRIME MINISTER: Your Majesty, the Weavers are strangers here. We don't know if we can trust them.

THE EMPEROR: Precisely, that is why we should have them here, in the palace, so we can keep an eye on them.

PRIME MINISTER: Very well, My Lord.

THE EMPEROR: What do you need in order to weave this marvelous cloth for me, Weavers?

WEAVERS: We need silk and golden thread that is the choicest in the land.

THE EMPEROR: Oh, we can arrange that.

WEAVER TWO: It is very expensive, Your Majesty, but only its fine quality is suited to Your Royal Highness.

THE EMPEROR: Expense is not a concern. I am the emperor and must have the best clothes in the world. I will pay you as much as you want and provide you with anything you need to realize this project.

WEAVERS: Thank you, Your Majesty, we are ready to work.

THE EMPEROR: Prime Minister, arrange the Weavers' workshop in the palace at once.

PRIME MINISTER: I will, My Lord.

PRIME MINISTER, *to the Weavers*: Follow me!

~ SCENE 2 ~

SET UP: The Weavers' Workshop

The Prime Minister leads the Weavers to their workshop.

PRIME MINISTER: Come inside, Weavers, it is your workshop now.

WEAVERS: We are coming, we are coming.

PRIME MINISTER: Here is your loom.

WEAVER TWO: A loom!

PRIME MINISTER: And a bag with the silk and golden thread you requested.

WEAVER ONE: Silk and golden thread. It is beautiful.

PRIME MINISTER: Also, here is your advance, three thousand golden ducats.

WEAVER ONE: Thank you.

WEAVER TWO: The Emperor is very generous.

PRIME MINISTER: He is, indeed. If you do good work, he will reward you even more, but if not...

WEAVERS: But if not?

PRIME MINISTER, (*is he joking or does he mean it?*): He will cut your heads off.

WEAVERS: Cut our heads off?!

PRIME MINISTER: Yes.

WEAVER TWO: You are joking, right?

PRIME MINISTER: You will see.

WEAVER ONE: We will do an excellent job.

PRIME MINISTER: You better, if you have a choice. Ha, ha, ha. Good night, gentlemen.

WEAVERS: Good night!

PRIME MINISTER: Ha, ha, ha.

The Prime Minister leaves. (Possibly locking the door with a key behind him.)

The Weavers are in a panic, running to and fro.

WEAVER TWO: Let's get out of here!

WEAVER ONE: No, no, no, we cannot get out of here.

WEAVER TWO: Why not?

WEAVER ONE: They are watching us.

WEAVER TWO: Who is watching us?

WEAVER ONE: The guards...

WEAVER TWO: Where are the guards?

WEAVER ONE: They are everywhere.

WEAVER TWO: We can sneak out!

WEAVER ONE: The people!

WEAVER TWO: What about the people?

WEAVER ONE: They are watching us too. Everybody is watching us. We can't get out now. We are trapped.

WEAVER TWO: What shall we do?

WEAVER ONE: Wait.

WEAVER TWO: What?

WEAVER ONE: Wait!

WEAVER TWO: I have to get out!

WEAVER ONE: Not now.

WEAVER TWO: Not now?

WEAVER ONE: No.

WEAVER TWO: When then?

WEAVER ONE: Later.

WEAVER TWO: We've got the money, silk and golden thread. Let's take it and get lost now.

WEAVER ONE: Wait, don't be so frantic.

WEAVER TWO: Wait for what?

WEAVER ONE: Wait for more.

WEAVER TWO: For more?

WEAVER ONE: For more money.

WEAVER TWO: Oh?! And how are we going to get it?

WEAVER ONE: The Prime Minister just said that The Emperor is going to pay us more.

WEAVER TWO: If we do a good job.

WEAVER ONE: We will.

WEAVER TWO: How?

WEAVER ONE: We will fake it.

WEAVER TWO: Fake it. I don't know how to fake it. I am not a real weaver.

WEAVER ONE: Neither am I!

WEAVER TWO: Let's get out of here before it's too late.

He is getting more frantic.

WEAVER ONE: Stop it! Be quiet!

WEAVER TWO: What?

WEAVER ONE: You are losing it.

WEAVER TWO: I am not losing it.

WEAVER ONE: Shh...

WEAVER TWO: Shh...

WEAVER ONE: Let's stick with our plan.

WEAVER TWO: Our plan?

WEAVER ONE: Let's pretend. Do you remember? You are good at pretending.

WEAVER TWO: Let's pretend to be weavers.

WEAVER ONE: Right!

WEAVER TWO: Right!

WEAVER ONE: I will set up the loom.

He is setting up the loom.

WEAVER TWO: What shall we do with the fine silk and golden thread?

WEAVER ONE: Hide it in our own knapsacks. We don't need it.

WEAVER TWO: We don't need it.

WEAVERS: We will pretend; we will pretend.

The Weavers pretend to weave on the empty loom.

~ TRANSITION ~

SET UP: Parallel action: The Weavers' Workshop and The Emperor's Chamber.

The NARRATOR steps center stage and speaks directly to the audience.

THE NARRATOR: They set up a loom and pretended to weave.

The Narrator with one magical gesture makes the Weavers freeze in a tableau, and with a second gesture, brings the action forth in The Emperor's chamber.

~ SCENE 3 ~

SET UP: The Emperor's Chamber/ The Weavers' Workshop.

THE NARRATOR: In the meantime…

THE EMPEROR: I would like to know how they are getting along!

PRIME MINISTER: Your Majesty, no one has seen the fabric yet.

THE EMPEROR: Why?

COUNCILOR: It is because those who tried to see it are either stupid or unfit for their office, or both.

THE EMPEROR: Why don't we send someone who is wise and the most suitable for the office then?

COUNCILOR: Who would that be, Your Majesty?

THE EMPEROR: I would go myself, but it would be better to send someone else the first time and see how he fares. I will send my faithful Prime Minister to see how the Weavers are getting along.

PRIME MINISTER: Me?

THE EMPEROR: Yes.

PRIME MINISTER: Why me?

THE EMPEROR: You will know how to judge the material because you are both clever and fit for your office, if any man is. Are you not?

PRIME MINISTER: Yes, I am, Your Majesty.

THE EMPEROR: Go on then and see what the Weavers have done so far.

PRIME MINISTER: Very well, My Lord. I am on my way.

The Narrator leads the Prime Minister to the Weavers' Workshop as if manipulating a puppet.

~ SCENE 4 ~

SET UP: The Weavers' Workshop

The Prime Minister looks at the empty loom.

THE NARRATOR: The good-natured old man stepped into the room where the Weavers were working and saw the empty loom.

PRIME MINISTER: How are you getting along, gentlemen?

WEAVERS: Thank you, well.

The Prime Minister closes his eyes and opens them again.

PRIME MINISTER: God preserve me! I cannot see a thing!

THE NARRATOR: Thought the Prime Minister but he didn't say it out loud.

WEAVER ONE: Please, step a little closer to the loom, Your Honor, so that you can admire the intricate patterns and marvelous colors of the cloth.

Both Weavers point to the empty loom. The Prime Minster comes closer and stares at the empty loom with his eyes wide open.

THE NARRATOR: The poor old Prime Minister opened his eyes as wide as he could; but it did not help, he still couldn't see a thing.

PRIME MINISTER: Am I stupid?

THE NARRATOR: He thought.

PRIME MINISTER, *speaking to the audience*: I can't believe it, but if it is so, it is best no one finds out about it. Or maybe I am not fit for my office. No, that is worse. I'd better not admit that I can't see what they are weaving.

WEAVER TWO: Tell us what you think of it.

PRIME MINISTER: It is beautiful.

WEAVER ONE: How do you like the patterns?

PRIME MINISTER: They are very lovely.

WEAVER TWO: How do you like the colors?

PRIME MINISTER: They are, they are...

WEAVER TWO: Pleasing?

PRIME MINISTER: Yes, very much so.

WEAVER ONE: Vibrant?

PRIME MINISTER: Yes, and vibrant.

WEAVER ONE: Touch the material and check its quality.

The Prime Minister touches the imaginary silk.

WEAVER TWO: Can you feel how soft it is?

PRIME MINISTER: Oh, yes, I can feel it. It's very soft.

WEAVER ONE: And pleasant to touch.

PRIME MINISTER: And pleasant to touch.

WEAVERS: Thank you for the compliment.

PRIME MINISTER: I shall tell The Emperor that it pleases me ever so much.

WEAVER TWO: Tell The Emperor also that we need more silk and golden thread.

PRIME MINISTER: You do?

WEAVER ONE: Yes. We have already used what you gave us, Your Honor.

PRIME MINISTER: I can see that. Anything else you need?

WEAVER TWO: Yes, more money.

PRIME MINISTER: Of course, you deserve more money for this...

WEAVER ONE: For this?

PRIME MINISTER: For this outstanding work. Yes, of course, I will tell The Emperor.

WEAVER TWO: Thank you.

PRIME MINISTER: Farewell.

The Prime Minister leaves. Weaver Two approaches the door to make sure that no one is listening.

WEAVER TWO: It works.

WEAVER ONE: It does.

They rub their hands with delight. They laugh and dance with joy. Then they lay back.

WEAVER ONE: We better get back to work.

WEAVER TWO: Why?

WEAVER ONE: Someone can see us.

WEAVER TWO: How?

WEAVER ONE: Through the window!

Weaver One checks the window.

WEAVER ONE: They can see us from the tower.

WEAVER TWO: Oh well, we better get back to work.

The Weavers go back to work; they pretend to weave.

The Narrator notices the Weavers working and makes a gesture to slow them down.

THE NARRATOR: Soon The Emperor sent another of his trusted councilors to see how the work was progressing.

~ SCENE 5 ~

SET UP: The Weavers' Workshop

The Emperor's Councilor enters the workshop and approaches the loom. The Narrator leads him with a gesture.

THE NARRATOR: He looked and looked just as the Prime Minister had, but since there was nothing to be seen, he didn't see anything.

COUNCILOR, *talking directly to the audience*: I am not stupid. I must be unfit for my office then. That is strange; but I'd better not admit it to anyone.

THE NARRATOR: Thought the Councilor but said nothing.

WEAVER ONE: Isn't it a marvelous piece of material?

COUNCILOR: Yes, it is very beautiful.

WEAVER TWO: How do you like its patterns and colors?

COUNCILOR: They are lovely.

WEAVER ONE: Touch the material and check its quality.

The Councilor touches the imaginary silk.

WEAVER TWO: Feel how soft it is.

COUNCILOR: Oh, yes, very soft.

WEAVER ONE: And pleasant to touch.

COUNCILOR: And pleasant to touch.

The Narrator makes a gesture to freeze the picture.

THE NARRATOR: The Weavers continued to describe the beauty of their imaginary cloth to The Emperor's Councilor exactly as they had done to the Prime Minister. And he repeated it word for word to The Emperor.

The Councilor goes to The Emperor's chamber.

~ SCENE 6 ~

SET UP: The Emperor's Chamber

The Emperor sits on the throne. The Councilor approaches.

COUNCILOR: Your Majesty, I have seen the cloth.

THE EMPEROR: Tell me, my Councilor, what was your impression?

COUNCILOR: I think it is the most charming piece of material I have ever seen.

THE EMPEROR: Oh, I must go see that wonderful cloth myself before it is removed from the loom.

THE NARRATOR: And so, he went.

THE EMPEROR: Follow me!

~ SCENE 7 ~

SET UP: The Weavers' Workshop

Attended by the most important people in the Empire, among them the Prime Minister and the Councilor, who had been there before, The Emperor enters the room where the Weavers are weaving furiously on their empty loom.

WEAVER ONE: Your Majesty is here.

WEAVER TWO: Such an honor.

The Weavers jump to their feet.

THE EMPEROR: How are you getting along, Weavers?

WEAVER ONE: We are getting along well, Your Majesty. Thank you very much for your patience. The cloth is almost done.

THE EMPEROR: Can I see it now, while the cloth is still on the loom?

WEAVER ONE: Yes, you can, Your Majesty. Please, here it is.

The Emperor, followed by the Prime Minister, the Councilor, and Courtiers, approaches the empty loom and looks at the cloth but he sees nothing. The Weavers demonstrate the cloth, acting as if it were there.

PRIME MINISTER: Isn't it magnifique?

COUNCILOR: Your Majesty, look at the intricate patterns of colors. How do you like them?

THE EMPEROR, *to the audience*: What?! I can't see a thing! Why, this is a disaster! Am I stupid? Am I unfit to be emperor? Oh, it is too horrible.

THE NARRATOR: Thought The Emperor. But aloud he said:

THE EMPEROR: It is exquisitely beautiful!

He nods his head and looks at the empty loom.

All the Courtiers who came with him stare and stare; but they see no more than The Emperor sees.

COURTIERS (*ad-lib*): It is Beautiful! Very Beautiful! Exquisite. It's lovely, very lovely! Wonderful! Admirable!

They all stop for a moment in exalted poses that express admiration and look at the imaginary cloth as if they were hypnotized.

WEAVER ONE: Your Majesty...

THE EMPEROR, *as if snapping out of it*: Yes?

WEAVER ONE: Do you approve of the quality of the fabric?

THE EMPEROR: Yes, I do. It is... (*a long moment of consternation*)...

COUNCILOR: Extraordinary, Your Majesty?

THE EMPEROR: Yes, it is extraordinary! I've never seen something like it before. It's hypnotizing.

PRIME MINISTER: Indeed, hypnotizing.

THE EMPEROR: Prime Minister!

PRIME MINISTER: Yes, My Lord.

THE EMPEROR: Fetch me my scepter!

A SERVANT brings his scepter on a pillow.

PRIME MINISTER: Here it is, Your Royal Highness!

THE EMPEROR: Kneel down, Weavers. Kneel down, don't be afraid. I am not going to behead you. Ha, ha, ha. They are scared. Ha, ha, ha. Kneel down!

The Weavers kneel down.

THE EMPEROR *places the scepter on the shoulder of Weaver One*: I give you the title "Royal Knight of the Loom."

THE EMPEROR *places the scepter on the shoulder of Weaver Two:* I give you the title "Royal Knight of the Loom."

The Emperor puts the scepter back on the pillow.

THE EMPEROR: Stand up, please.

The Weavers stand up.

THE EMPEROR: You are masters of your craft, not just weavers but artists who create beauty. (*applause*)

THE EMPEROR: Everyone in the court admires the cloth you wove. (*more applause*)

THE EMPEROR: I want you to cut and sew clothes for me made from this miraculous cloth. And I will wear them in the procession at the next great celebration, so all the subjects can see and admire me. (*more applause*)

WEAVER ONE: Your Majesty, when is the next great procession?

THE EMPEROR: It is tomorrow, gentlemen.

WEAVER TWO: Tomorrow?

THE EMPEROR: Yes, I must have it tomorrow. I am so excited. I cannot imagine myself in anything else but in clothes made of this marvelous cloth you have woven. Can you make it on time?

WEAVER ONE: Yes, Your Majesty. We will work all night to make it on time.

THE EMPEROR: Good!

WEAVER TWO: Let us take your measurements now, Your Highness.

THE EMPEROR: Please, do... Prime Minister, dismiss the court.

PRIME MINISTER: The court is dismissed!

The Courtiers withdraw from the room.

The Weavers measure The Emperor's body with a measuring tape and write it down on a pad.

WEAVER TWO, *while measuring The Emperor's shoulders*: Fourteen inches.

THE EMPEROR: Make it eighteen.

WEAVER ONE *makes a note*: Shoulders, eighteen inches in width.

WEAVER TWO *measures the waist*: Forty-six inches.

WEAVER ONE: Waist: forty-six inches in girth.

THE EMPEROR: Make it tighter, please.

WEAVER ONE: Yes, Your Majesty, we will make it to appear much tighter: thirty-six, let's say.

THE EMPEROR: That's sounds right.

WEAVER TWO *measures the leg*: Thirty-one in length.

THE EMPEROR: I will wear high heels.

The Emperor stands on tiptoes.

WEAVER ONE: Thirty-three?

THE EMPEROR: Very high heels!

WEAVER ONE: Thirty-five inches then.

WEAVER TWO *measures the arm*: Twenty-four inches.

WEAVER ONE *takes a note*: Sleeves in length: twenty-four inches.

WEAVER TWO: That's it.

WEAVER ONE: Got it! Your Majesty, that will be all for now.

THE EMPEROR: Thank you, gentlemen.

The Emperor exits.

WEAVER ONE: We better get to work at once.

THE NARRATOR: The night before the procession, the two swindlers didn't sleep at all.

Four ROYAL SERVANTS carry four candelabras with candles. They hold them and light the room throughout the entire scene.

The Weavers mime making clothes.

THE NARRATOR: They pretended to take the cloth from the loom; they cut the air with their big scissors and sewed with needles without thread. At last, they announced:

WEAVERS (*center stage*): The Emperor's clothes are ready!

ECHOING VOICES: The Emperor's clothes are ready! The Emperor's clothes are ready.

~ SCENE 8 ~

SET UP: The Emperor's Clothes Closet

The Weavers bring The Emperor's clothes to his closet. The Emperor stands in front of the mirror.

THE EMPEROR: Bring them to me!

WEAVER ONE: Will Your Imperial Majesty be so gracious as to take off your clothes?

THE EMPEROR: I will!

He takes his clothes off; his personal Dressers assists him.

THE EMPEROR: Take them and throw them away. I never wear the same clothes twice.

DRESSER ONE: As you wish, Your Majesty.

THE EMPEROR: Show me what you have, gentlemen?

The Weavers lift their arms as if they are holding something in their hands.

WEAVER ONE: These are the trousers.

WEAVER TWO: This is the robe, and here is the train.

THE EMPEROR: How do I put them on?

WEAVER ONE: Over there by the big mirror, we shall help you put them on.

THE NARRATOR: The Emperor did as he was told; and the swindlers acted as if they were dressing him in the clothes they should have made.

Weaver One helps The Emperor put on imaginary trousers.

WEAVER ONE: And now the robe.

He helps The Emperor put on the imaginary robe.

WEAVER ONE: Good.

WEAVER TWO: Excellent!

The Emperor regards himself in the mirror.

THE EMPEROR: How does it fit?

WEAVER ONE: It fits perfectly, Your Highness.

WEAVER TWO: As if it were your own skin, Your Majesty.

THE EMPEROR: How do I look?

WEAVER ONE: You look sublime.

WEAVER TWO: Truly yourself, Your Highness.

WEAVER ONE: How does it feel, Your Highness?

THE EMPEROR: It feels so light, as if I had on almost nothing.

WEAVER ONE: That is their special virtue. We've made the cloth from a thread as delicate as a spider's web, Your Imperial Majesty.

THE NARRATOR: The Emperor stood in front of the mirror admiring the clothes he couldn't see.

THE EMPEROR: Well, I am dressed. Aren't my clothes becoming?

The Emperor turns around once more in front of the mirror, pretending to study his finery.

COURTIER ONE: Oh, how they suit you!

COURTIER TWO: A perfect fit!

COURTIER THREE: What colors!

COURTIER FOUR: What patterns!

THE NARRATOR: Exclaimed all the Courtiers; but they saw nothing, for there was nothing to be seen.

THE MASTER OF CEREMONY, *announcing with pomp:* The new clothes are magnificent!

They all bow to The Emperor.

THE EMPEROR: Attach the train!

WEAVER ONE: Very well, Your Majesty!

THE NARRATOR: Finally, around his waist they tied the long train, which two of his most noble Courtiers were to carry.

The Weavers attach the imaginary train on The Emperor.

WEAVER TWO: The train is laid down, Your Highness!

THE EMPEROR: I am ready to go. Take my train! Go on.

The TWO COURTIERS of The Imperial Bedchamber fumble on the floor, trying to find the train which they are supposed to carry.

THE NARRATOR: They didn't dare admit that they didn't see anything, so they pretended to pick up the train and held their hands as if they were carrying it.

THE MASTER OF CEREMONY: The crimson canopy, under which Your Imperial Majesty is to walk, is waiting outside.

~ SCENE 9 ~

SET UP: The Street

The Emperor walks in the procession under his crimson canopy.

The TOWN FOLK line the street.

THE TOWN FOLK: What a magnificent robe! And the train! How well The Emperor's clothes suit him!

The Emperor strikes an impressive pose; the Town Folk applaud him. The Narrator freezes them all into a tableau with one magical gesture.

THE NARRATOR: None of them were willing to admit that they hadn't seen a thing; for if anyone did, then he was either stupid or unfit for the job he held. Curiously, never before had The Emperor's clothes been such a success. Until. Look what happened:

The Narrator brings the Town Folk and the Courtiers into motion with one magical gesture. The procession continues.

A LITTLE CHILD: But he doesn't have anything on!

FATHER: Listen to the innocent one. A little child says that he has nothing on.

THE TOWN FOLK *whisper*: The child says that he has nothing on. Nothing on? The child says he has nothing on. He has nothing on. Nothing on.

THE FATHER *shouts*: The child says he has nothing on! He has nothing on! The Emperor is naked.

COURTIERS *begin to whisper and then shout*: He has nothing on! The Emperor is naked!

All of them stop and look at The Emperor. Some of them point at him with their fingers. The Emperor shivers. He wants to hide.

THE EMPEROR: What a shame! I am no one without the clothes. It is terrible. Do something!

PRIME MINISTER: Protect The Emperor: Royal Guards, Courtiers, form a cordon around His Highness.

Courtiers cover The Emperor with their bodies; Guards protect him by pointing their rifles with bayonets at the crowd.

THE MASTER OF CEREMONY: The child is lying!

FATHER: The child speaks his mind. He is not lying. He is telling the truth.

THE MASTER OF CEREMONY: The child is politically incorrect! You raised a monster, shame on you!

PRIME MINISTER: Guards, seize the child and his father.

The Royal Guards make a move toward the Child and his Father. The Father stands in front of his son to protect him.

FATHER: Believe the child, he is innocent.

When the guards are about to seize the Child and his Father, the Narrator steps in and freezes the action by making one magical gesture.

THE NARRATOR: Stop it right here! That is not how the original story, written by Hans Christian Andersen, ended. No one knew the term, "politically correct" yet. It is a modern idea. Let's not get carried away with our zeal for censorship but do it the way it was written. *(To the actors.)* Back up a little bit, please. Go!

The actors back up to the moment the Child says:

A LITTLE CHILD: But he doesn't have anything on!

FATHER: Listen to the innocent one. A little child says that he has nothing on.

THE TOWN FOLK *whisper*: The child says that he has nothing on. Nothing on? The child says he has nothing on.

THE TOWN FOLK, a*ll the people shout*: He has nothing on!

THE EMPEROR: I must bear it until the procession is over.

The Emperor walks on. His entourage follows.

THE NARRATOR: And he walked even more proudly, and the two gentlemen of The Imperial Bedchamber went on carrying the train that wasn't there.

~ THE END ~

~ ~ ~

~ The Maiden without Hands ~

~ A Play ~

by

Christopher Vened

Based on

A Grimms' Fairy Tale of the Same Title

~ CAST OF CHARACTERS ~

<u>The Narrator</u>: He/She speaks directly to the audience while narrating the story and invoking the action with gestures and movement at the same time.

<u>The Maiden</u>: An innocent girl whose father sells her to The Devil

<u>The Miller</u>: The Maiden's Father

<u>The Miller's Wife</u>: The Maiden's Mother

<u>The Devil</u>: He harasses The Maiden

<u>The Angel</u>: She protects The Maiden

<u>The Gardener</u>: He finds The Maiden in the Royal Garden

<u>The King</u>: He marries The Maiden

<u>Two Courtiers</u>: In the Royal Castle

<u>The King's Mother</u>: A compassionate Old Queen

<u>The Messenger</u>: He delivers wrong letters to The King

<u>The Chamberlain</u>: He assists The King at the War Camp

<u>The Old Man</u>: The Maiden meets him in the forest

<u>The Son</u>: The Maiden's Son whom she calls, "Sorrowful"

<u>Three Water Spirits</u>: In the Royal Garden

~ SCENES ~

The Miller's House

The Forest

The Royal Garden

The King's Palace

A Brook

A Cottage in the Forest

~ TIME ~

Mythological

~ PROLOGUE ~

THE NARRATOR: Ladies and Gentlemen, this story is titled "The Maiden Without Hands," and it is about the fears and hopes a girl experiences during puberty. At times this story is like a nightmare, at others, like a beautiful dream. Nothing is realistic about it, but everything is true. Please, enjoy the story.

~ SCENE 1 ~

SET UP: The Forest

THE MILLER gathers wood in the forest. He cuts dry branches from a tree.

An old man, THE DEVIL, approaches.

THE DEVIL: Why do you torment yourself with chopping wood, Miller?

THE MILLER: I fell into poverty and now I have to gather wood in the forest.

THE DEVIL: I will make you rich if you will promise me that whatever is standing behind your mill will be mine.

THE MILLER: Behind my mill?

THE DEVIL: Yes.

THE MILLER: What can that be but my apple tree?

THE DEVIL: Whatever is there now I will take it in three years from today.

THE MILLER: That's a deal, old man!

THE DEVIL: Sign your promise in writing, Miller, to make our contract binding.

The Devil mimes pulling out a feather pen, a bottle of ink, and then unrolls parchment paper.

THE MILLER: I will. *He writes the following words on the parchment as he speaks them aloud:*

If you make me rich, I will give you everything that stands behind my mill.

THE DEVIL, *prompting him:* Right now.

THE MILLER, *writing and speaking*: ... right now.

THE DEVIL, *prompting him*: Sign it.

THE MILLER, *writing and speaking*: Miller.

He signs the contract with gusto. The Devil rolls the contract and puts it into his pocket.

THE DEVIL: In three years, I'll come and fetch what's mine!

The Devil goes away.

THE MILLER *shouts after him*: If you deliver!

THE DEVIL: I will deliver. Go home, Miller. And you will find that you are rich.

The Devil disappears.

THE MILLER: We will see.

THE MILLER *turns to the audience*: That was strange, wasn't it? Like a dream. Well, in case it was just a dream I'll take this bundle of wood and carry it home.

He picks up the bundle and flings it on his shoulders.

~ SCENE 2 ~

SET UP: The Miller's House

THE MAIDEN, The Miller's daughter, is sweeping out the yard behind the mill. Then she stops, picks an apple from the tree, and eats it.

The Miller returns home; his WIFE comes out to meet him.

THE MILLER'S WIFE: Tell me, husband, how did all this wealth suddenly get into our house?

THE MILLER: Did it?

THE MILLER'S WIFE: Yes. All at once I've discovered our chests and boxes are full. Nobody's brought anything, and I don't know how it's all happened.

THE MILLER: It's from a stranger I met in the forest.

THE MILLER'S WIFE: A stranger? What do you mean?

THE MILLER: He promised me great wealth if I agreed in writing to give him what's behind our mill. We can certainly spare the large apple tree.

He points to the tree.

THE MILLER'S WIFE: Oh, husband! That was The Devil! He didn't mean the apple tree but our daughter, who was behind the mill sweeping out the yard.

THE MILLER: Oh, my God, I sold my own daughter unwittingly.

THE MILLER'S WIFE: Now what are we going to do, husband?

THE MILLER: There is nothing we can do. I've signed a contract with The Devil. It cannot be undone.

THE MILLER'S WIFE: Oh, my God, have mercy on our daughter.

THE MAIDEN, *overhearing the conversation*: Father, Mother, do not lament. I will never go to The Devil. He has no power over me.

THE MILLER'S WIFE: Daughter, The Devil has no power over you yet because you are an innocent child. But he will come to fetch you in three years, when you become a woman.

THE MAIDEN: Oh, Mother! I will always remain your child, I promise.

THE MILLER'S WIFE *is moved and cries*: You are naive. It melts my heart.

THE MAIDEN: Father, will you protect me when The Devil comes?

THE MILLER: It is beyond my power, daughter! The Devil is stronger than I.

THE MAIDEN: Who is stronger than The Devil, Father?

THE MILLER: God is stronger than The Devil.

The Maiden turns toward the audience and takes it in.

THE MAIDEN, *toward the audience*: Then, I will ask God for protection.

THE MILLER'S WIFE, *from behind*: Do my daughter, do.

THE MILLER, *to his wife*: Let's go inside the house and enjoy our riches.

The Miller and his Wife go inside the house. The Maiden stays on the stage.

~ SCENE 3 ~

SET UP: The Miller's House - Yard

The Maiden kneels and prays in the yard.

THE NARRATOR, *to the audience*: She lived the three years piously, worshiping God and without sin.

The Maiden picks an apple from the apple tree and eats it. It tastes like a forbidden fruit and makes her sick to her stomach. She senses The Devil is coming to get her.

THE NARRATOR, *to the audience*: When the time was up and the day came when the evil one was to get her, she washed herself clean and drew a circle around herself with chalk.

The Maiden mimes washing herself clean in the nearby river. Afterward she draws a circle around herself with chalk. And then she kneels inside the center of the circle, folds her hands, and prays. It has a ritualistic feel.

The Devil comes to fetch her, but he cannot approach her. She is protected inside the circle by some invisible force. When The Devil tries to cross the circle, he is electrocuted. He makes a few attempts to cross the line of the circle but is repulsed with the invisible force and jumps away with ugly screams of pain.

THE DEVIL *shouts:* Miller, Miller, come out of the house!

The Miller comes out of the house; his Wife eventually follows.

THE MILLER: Who are you stranger? And why are you making such a fuss so early in the morning?

THE DEVIL: Don't you remember me and the contract you made with me in the forest?

THE MILLER: I do remember.

THE DEVIL: Do you enjoy the gold and wealth I gave you?

MILLER: Yes, I do.

THE DEVIL: I came to collect my due. Your daughter is mine now.

The Devil reaches for The Maiden, but he is electrocuted again. He screams with pain.

THE DEVIL: Tell your daughter not to resist me. Tell her that she is mine, Miller.

THE MILLER: Daughter, it's time to go. Do not resist. Go with him. He is your husband.

THE MAIDEN: He is The Devil, Father. I will not go with him.

THE MILLER: He is not The Devil, Daughter, just a man.

THE MAIDEN: Father, can't you see? Look at his clubbed left foot. He has a hoof. He is The Devil.

The Devil hides his left foot behind him, trying to stand straight. The Miller looks at his foot. They laugh it off.

THE MILLER: You are imagining things. Don't be afraid of him. He will take you to his home and take care of you. Go my Daughter, go. Its time.

THE MAIDEN, *with a pleading gesture*: Father, do not give me away to The Devil. I implore you.

The Devil reaches for The Maiden again but is repulsed by the invisible force even more. He screams in pain.

THE DEVIL: I cannot take her because she is too clean and pure. Take water away from her, Miller. Do it, Miller. Take water away from her. Make her unclean.

THE MILLER'S WIFE: Husband, do not give our daughter away. She is so young, still a child. Let her stay with us longer.

THE MILLER: She is already fifteen years old. When we married, you were merely twelve. Were you too young then?

THE MILLER'S WIFE: They were different times then.

The Devil strikes The Miller's Wife as if with lightening. It incapacitates her, she convulses, becomes paralyzed, and collapses. Then she goes away distressed.

THE DEVIL: Do what I tell you or I will strike you as I did her, Miller.

The Miller is frightened and takes the bucket of water away from The Maiden. The Maiden folds her hands in a praying gesture and cries. The Devil reaches for her but is repulsed with the invisible force again. This time the force is so strong that he falls on the ground. It makes him mad.

THE DEVIL: She washes herself in her own tears, I still can't take her. It makes me mad. Chop off her hands, Miller, so she can't wash herself anymore. Do it.

THE MILLER: How could I chop off my own child's hands?!

THE DEVIL: If you do not do it, then you will be mine.

The Devil makes a threatening gesture to strike The Miller.

THE MILLER, *terrified*: Please, do not strike me. I will obey you. I will do it.

THE DEVIL: Go to her and do it then.

The Miller goes close to the girl.

THE MILLER: My child, if I do not chop off both of your hands, then The Devil will take me away. Help me in my need and forgive me for the evil that I am going to do to you.

The Miller's Wife reappears.

THE MILLER'S WIFE: Husband, don't do it.

THE MILLER: Wife, I must do it. I promised. I gave my word.

THE MILLER'S WIFE: You gave your word to The Devil.

The Devil strikes her with lightening. It incapacitates her momentarily, but she overcomes her weakness and stands up to The Devil again.

THE MILLER: We got the gold as we were promised. I have to keep my part of the bargain.

THE MILLER'S WIFE: Give the gold back.

THE MILLER: I can't.

THE MILLER'S WIFE: You can.

THE MILLER: We would lose everything that we have. It would ruin us. I don't want to be poor again. We will all end up on the street, asking for alms like beggars.

THE MILLER'S WIFE: We can work as hired hands. A man can always find work and earn a living if he wants to.

THE MILLER: I don't want to be a pauper. I don't want to be poor.

THE MILLER'S WIFE: The gold has changed you, my husband.

THE MILLER: I don't want us to be poor again. It will ruin us.

THE MILLER'S WIFE: You are not good anymore.

The Devil strikes her with lightening again. She falls dead.

THE MILLER: My wife has just died. With a curse on her lips. Why don't you leave us alone? Go away.

THE DEVIL, *pointing at The Maiden*: It is all her fault. Chop off her hands.

THE MAIDEN: Dear Father, do with me what you will. I am your child. I don't want to lose you.

She stretches both hands to let her father chop them off. The Miller chops off her hands with an imaginary axe. The Maiden screams and withdraws her hands. She hides them behind her back or between her legs then pulls them out folded in fists. She looks at the stumps covered in blood. She cries violently, with black despair. Her tears fall on her stumps and clean them. She hides her hands behind her back for a moment. Then she pulls them out entirely clean and folds them together in a gesture of praying. There is no blood on them anymore. It is a ritual of puberty.

The Devil comes again to take her. But he can't because she is clean.

THE DEVIL: I can't take her now. She is beyond my reach. You can keep her, Miller. You have fulfilled your part of our bargain. But I will be back!

The Devil departs.

THE MILLER, *to his daughter*: I have gained great wealth through you. I shall take care of you in splendor as long as you live.

THE MAIDEN: I cannot remain here. I will go away. Compassionate people will give me as much as I need.

The Maiden goes away.

~ SCENE 4 ~

SET UP: On the Road

The Narrator approaches The Maiden and interacts with her. She raises The Maiden up with a gentle gesture and then leads her away. They go on a metaphysical journey, which is like a dream.

THE NARRATOR: Then she had her mutilated arms tied to her back, and at sunrise she set forth, walking the entire day until it was night.

As The Narrator speaks, she directs The Maiden to perform actions. She puts her hands behind her back to be tied and then keeps them there as if her arms are tied. She begins her journey. She walks in one place, facing the audience - it's a mime walk.

~ SCENE 5 ~

SET UP: The Royal Garden

THE NARRATOR: She came to a royal garden, and by the light of the moon she saw that inside there were trees full of beautiful fruits. But she could not get inside because it was surrounded by water.

THREE OR MORE WATER SPIRITS appear behind The Maiden. They animate the movement of the water with their hands. First, they touch the surface, skimming it gently with their palms and fingers, then they undulate the wave shapes, gradually involving the whole body and becoming fluid, swaying from side to side in an ebbing and flowing rhythm.

When The Maiden approaches the Water Spirts, they become demonic like the ghosts of drowned girls. It is a nightmare. Frightened to cross the water, The Maiden withdraws.

The Maiden kneels and prays to God.

While she is praying, the Water Spirits become pacified. Now their floating movement induces the sensation of calm, poise, and tranquility.

THE MAIDEN, *praying*: God, I kneel before you as I did many times before, please, have mercy on me. I have walked the entire day without eating a bite. I am hungry! If I don't eat anything, I will perish. Please, God, hear my supplication. I don't want to die. I want to live. (*She cries.*)

THE ANGEL approaches The Maiden from behind and raises her up with invisible power, without touching The Maiden but by making gestures in slow motion.

THE ANGEL *whispers*: Stand up, stand up! Come on. Follow me to the garden.

The Maiden stands up and The Angel leads her to the garden. They walk in unison in slow motion like spirits. They approach an imaginary PEAR TREE.

The Maiden steps up to the tree and looks with hunger at a pear but is not able to reach it. The Angel bends an imaginary bough and picks a pear for her.

THE ANGEL: Eat it.

The Maiden eats the pear from The Angel's hand.

THE GARDENER sees it all happen but when he wants to approach The Maiden, The Angel stands in his way and with a hand-motion sends The Gardener away. He backs off.

Then, The Maiden goes and lies down in the brush.

THE MAIDEN: Thank you, God. I am full now and sleepy. I will lie and rest in that brush, so no one will see me.

THE ANGEL: Go and lie down.

The Maiden lies down in the brush. The Angel soothes her to sleep.

THE ANGEL: Sleep now. Sleep!

THE MAIDEN: Thank you, God, for food. I am full now and sleepy. I feel safe here, as if an angel held me in her arms.

THE ANGEL: Shh. It's time to sleep.

The Maiden falls asleep; The Angel withdraws.

~ SCENE 6 ~

SET UP: The Royal Garden; Morning

THE NARRATOR: The King, who owned this garden, came the next morning.

THE KING and The Gardener approach the pear tree. The King counts the fruit.

THE KING: One of the pears is missing. It is not lying under the tree, but has somehow disappeared. What happened to it?

THE GARDENER: Last night a spirit came here. It had no hands and ate one of the pears with its mouth.

THE KING: How did the spirit get across the water? And where did it go?

THE GARDENER: Someone dressed in snow-white came from heaven and closed the head gate so the spirit could walk through the moat. Because it must have been an angel, I was afraid, and I asked no questions, and I did not call out. After the spirit ate the pear, it went away again.

THE KING: If what you said is true, I will keep watch with you tonight.

The King and The Gardener step away.

THE NARRATOR: After it was dark, The King entered the garden again, and he and The Gardener sat down under the tree and kept watch.

The King and The Gardener re-enter and sit under the tree. The Narrator directs them with suggestive gestures, but she is invisible to them.

THE NARRATOR: At midnight the girl came creeping out of the brush, stepped up to the tree, and again ate of a pear with her mouth. An angel dressed in white was standing next to her.

The Maiden does as The Narrator describes, and The Angel assists her.

The King walks toward The Maiden; The Angel beckons him, encouraging him to come closer.

THE KING: Have you come from God or from the world? Are you a spirit or a human?

THE MAIDEN: I am not a spirit, but a poor human who has been abandoned by everyone except God.

She kneels in humility.

THE KING: Even if you have been abandoned by the whole world, I will not abandon you.

THE MAIDEN: My Lord!

She says it while looking up to heaven.

THE KING: You are so beautiful and pure. What are you doing here, in my garden?

THE MAIDEN: I came to eat your pears.

THE KING: My pears?

THE MAIDEN: Forgive me, Your Highness, but I was hungry. I walked the whole day without food and had no place to go.

THE KING: Where are you going?

THE MAIDEN: I don't know.

THE KING: You don't know?

THE MAIDEN *whispers:* No.

THE KING: Where are you coming from?

THE MAIDEN: I am running away from my home.

THE KING: Come, give me your hand, I will take you to my castle.

THE MAIDEN: I cannot give you my hand, Your Highness.

THE KING: Why not?

THE MAIDEN: I don't have hands.

THE KING: What happened?

THE MAIDEN: My father chopped them off.

THE KING: Why did he do such a cruel deed to his own daughter?

THE MAIDEN: For gold. He sold them for gold.

THE KING: Show me your hands.

THE MAIDEN: Your Highness, they look gruesome. There are no hands, only two bloody stumps.

THE KING: Let me see them.

The Maiden pulls out her hands. They are completely intact.
The King touches them, then holds them.

THE MAIDEN *withdraws her hands*: Don't touch them, My Lord. They are my shame and anguish.

THE KING: Don't be ashamed, don't worry anymore. I will give you a new pair of hands.

THE MAIDEN: How?

THE KING: I will order golden hands made for you. Come home with me, to the Royal Castle. Will you?

THE MAIDEN: I will.

The King takes The Maiden to the castle.

~ SCENE 7 ~

SET UP: The Royal Castle

THE NARRATOR: He took her home with him to his Royal Castle, and because she was so beautiful and pure he loved her with all his heart. He had golden hands made for her and took her as his wife.

The Narrator's speech is illustrated in a few tableaus that are in motion. A) The King brings The Maiden to the castle and presents her to the court. B) The King calls with a gesture for a COURTIER to bring the golden hands made for The Maiden, which are actually a pair of gloves. The Courtier brings the golden gloves on a pillow. The King ceremoniously takes them and puts them on The Maiden's hands.

THE KING: I had golden hands made for you. Here they are. Put them on and become my queen.

The Maiden hesitates.

THE KING: Let me help you.

THE MAIDEN: Please, do.

The King puts the golden gloves on The Maiden's hands. She looks at her new hands, moves her fingers, makes a few grasping motions, and demonstrates them.

THE MAIDEN: I've got new hands.

THE KING: Do you like them?

THE MAIDEN: Yes, I do. They look real. And I can move them, and I can touch with them.

THE KING: Now you are my wife and The Queen!

He kneels on one knee in front of her. Then she kneels on two knees in front of him. It shall be performed as a marriage ritual.

THE MAIDEN: My husband and The King, I am the happiest woman in the world!

He takes her by the hand and leads her to the throne.

THE KING: Come and sit with me on the throne.

They sit and then The King and The Queen freeze on the throne.

THE NARRATOR: After a year, The King had to go out into the battlefield, and he left the young Queen in the care of his mother.

THE KING: Mother, when she has the child, support her and take good care of her.

THE KING'S MOTHER: Of course, I will.

THE KING: And immediately send me the news in a letter.

THE KING'S MOTHER: I will. Don't worry. She is in good care, my son.

THE KING, *to The Maiden*: Farewell, my love.

He reaches his hand (palm up) toward her; she puts her hand on his. Then, they do the same with the other hand.

THE MAIDEN: These hands are cold. I cannot feel that I touch you.

THE KING *kisses her hand*: They are not cold. You imagine it.

THE MAIDEN: Kiss my lips, my husband, so I can feel you, they are soft and warm.

They kiss.

THE KING: Farewell, my love.

THE MAIDEN: Farewell!

The King departs.

SET UP: Many different short scenes in various locations.

THE NARRATOR: She gave birth to a beautiful son.

The Maiden holds a baby in her hands.

THE NARRATOR: The King's Mother quickly wrote this in a letter, giving the joyful news to The King.

The King's Mother writes a letter (miming) and then gives it to THE MESSENGER.

The Messenger mimes mounting a horse and takes off.

THE NARRATOR: On the way, The Messenger stopped at a brook to rest. Tired from his long journey, he fell asleep.

The Messenger rides a horse, then stops and dismounts center stage. He drinks water from a brook, then he rests and falls asleep.

THE NARRATOR: While he slept, The Devil came to him. The Devil still wanted to harm the Pious Queen, so he stole the letter from The Messenger's satchel and put in its place one that stated that The Queen had brought a changeling into the world.

The Devil comes, steals the letter, and reads it with derision. It is a mime – the letter is imaginary, and The Devil shows what he is reading with mimicry and gestures. Then, he crumples the letter, tears it into pieces, and eats it. Then he vomits it with disgust.

Next, The Devil writes a new letter with an imaginary pen while miming its content. It is a wickedly delicious mime.

Next, The Devil exchanges the letter. Then, he goes away.

The Messenger wakes up and continues his journey. He arrives at the WAR CAMP and delivers the letter to The King.

THE MESSENGER *kneels and bows*: I bring a letter from The King's Mother.

THE CHAMBERLAIN: Give it to me.

The Chamberlain takes the letter and brings it to The King.

THE CHAMBERLAIN: A letter from your mother, Your Highness.

THE KING *reads the letter to the audience:* "The Queen has brought a changeling into the world. He does not look like your child. He is deformed and has ugly features. He has a low brow, short neck, thick fingers and bowlegs. He is hairy all over his body like an animal. He is a monster."

The King gives the letter back to The Chamberlain, who reads it, while The King saddened by the news, becomes despondent.

THE CHAMBERLAIN: My Lord, what is your answer to the Queen Mother's letter?

THE KING *dictates*: Please, write to my mother: Mother, the child you describe as an ugly monster is my son. I take him as he is, for he is a gift from heaven. Do not let bad thoughts come to you. Protect my son and his mother. I cherish them from afar, but my return is imminent.

The Chamberlain writes down The King's words. When The King is done dictating, he waves to The Messenger.

THE KING: You may send the letter now.

THE CHAMBERLAIN: Yes, My Lord.

He folds and gives the letter to The Messenger.

THE CHAMBERLAIN: Deliver this letter to The King's Mother.

THE MESSENGER: I will.

The Messenger mounts a horse and takes off.

THE NARRATOR: The Messenger returned with this letter, but he rested at the same place, and again fell asleep.

The Messenger falls asleep.

THE NARRATOR: The Devil came again and placed a different letter in his bag.

The Devil picks up and reads The King's letter with detestation. Then he writes a new letter with utter malice. All of it is expressed in mime.

THE NARRATOR: This letter told The King's Mother that she should kill The Queen and her child.

The Devil goes away. The Messenger wakes up; looks to the sun, realizes it's late, jumps to his feet, mounts the horse, and rides away in a hurry.

~ SCENE 9 ~

SET UP: The King's Palace

THE NARRATOR: The Messenger delivers the letter to The King's Mother.

THE MESSENGER *kneels and bows:* I bring a letter from The King to The King's Mother!

The Maiden makes a start in anticipation and then backs off.

THE KING'S MOTHER: Stand up and give it to me.

The Messenger gives her the letter.

THE MESSENGER: Your Majesty, here it is, the letter from The King!

THE KING'S MOTHER: Very well!

She takes the letter and dismisses The Messenger. He withdraws.

THE MESSENGER: Your Majesty.

THE KING'S MOTHER: Let me read the letter aloud, it is from your husband.

THE MAIDEN: Please, do! I am very excited to hear from him.

THE KING'S MOTHER *reads the letter*: "Mother, I married a witch. I don't want her child. Kill him and throw him in the river. Kill his mother, too. I don't want to see them. Keep The Queen's tongue and the child's eyes as proof."

THE MAIDEN: This cannot be my husband's words!

THE KING'S MOTHER: War changes men. It makes them bloody beasts.

THE MAIDEN: Have mercy on me. Do not kill me and my son. I never wanted to be a queen.

THE KING'S MOTHER: Don't be afraid, I cannot have you killed, as The King has ordered, but you can no longer stay here.

THE MAIDEN: Where shall I go?

THE KING'S MOTHER: Go out into the wide world with your child and never come back.

The Maiden is shocked. She looks up to heaven, resigning herself to God. THE NANNY brings the child. As in a trance, The Maiden approaches her and takes her child in her arms and hands. But she drops him on the ground.

THE KING'S MOTHER: You dropped the child.

THE MAIDEN: He is all right.

THE KING'S MOTHER: Take your son and hold him with care.

The King's Mother picks up the child and gives him to The Maiden. But she does not take him.

THE MAIDEN: I cannot take him and hold him with these golden hands that I've gotten from my husband. They are hard and cold. I cannot feel anything with them! (*The Maiden becomes hysterical.*) I don't want them anymore. I will do without them.

She takes off her golden hands and puts them on the throne.

THE KING'S MOTHER: How are you going to carry your child without hands?

THE MAIDEN: Tie him to my back.

The King's Mother ties The Maiden's child onto her back.

THE NARRATOR: The King's Mother tied The Queen's child onto her back, and the poor woman went away with weeping eyes.

The Maiden walks away.

~ SCENE 10 ~

SET UP: The Forest

The Maiden walks in the forest. It is shown through a mime walk in one place facing the audience.

THE NARRATOR: In the evening, she came to a place in a thick forest where a good old man was sitting by a spring.

THE OLD MAN sits on the ground with his eyes closed, meditating. The Maiden approaches him.

THE MAIDEN: Old Man, are you awake?

THE OLD MAN: Yes, I am.

The Old Man opens his eyes.

THE MAIDEN: Could you be so kindhearted as to hold my child to my breast until I have nursed him?

THE OLD MAN: Why would you not hold your child to your breast yourself?

THE MAIDEN: I don't have hands to hold him.

THE OLD MAN: What happened to your hands?

THE MAIDEN: My father chopped them off and sold them to The Devil for gold.

THE OLD MAN: Show me your maimed hands.

The Maiden shows The Old Man her hands (which are perfectly intact and healthy.) The Old Man touches them.

THE OLD MAN: I can cure them.

THE MAIDEN: How?

THE OLD MAN: Go to that thick tree over there and wrap your maimed arms around it three times.

THE MAIDEN: What kind of tree is there that can cure my hands?

THE OLD MAN: It is the Tree of Life. It has stood over there for nearly six thousand years. Go and embrace it.

The Maiden goes and embraces an imaginary thick tree, three times. Then she looks at her hands. She is now able to see them.

THE MAIDEN: My hands! They've grown back. It is a miracle!

She touches one hand with the other, exploring them and checking if they are real.

THE MAIDEN: Look, they are real.

She shows her hands to The Old Man.

THE OLD MAN: Now you can use them, Queen.

THE MAIDEN: Yes, I can! How did you know that I am a queen?

THE OLD MAN: That is not important. Come with me now.

THE MAIDEN: Where?

THE OLD MAN: I will show you the cottage where you will live with your son.

The Maiden stands up and follows The Old Man to the cottage.

THE NARRATOR: She stayed in this cottage for seven years and was well taken care of.

~ SCENE 11 ~

SET UP: The King's Palace

THE NARRATOR: In the meantime, The King had finally come back home from the battlefield, and the first thing he wanted to do was to see his wife and their child.

The King comes home and sees his mother.

THE KING: Mother, where is my wife and my child?

THE KING'S MOTHER: Why do you ask for them?

THE KING: I want to see them at once. Why don't they come to greet me?

THE KING'S MOTHER: You wicked man, why did you write to me that I was to put two innocent souls to death?

THE KING: I did not write such a wicked thing.

THE KING'S MOTHER: Here is your letter. Read it.

She shows him the letter that The Devil had forged.

THE KING: What have you done, Mother?

THE KING'S MOTHER: I did what you ordered. Here is the proof: your wife's tongue that I cut off and your son's eyes I pulled out.

She shows him the proof.

THE KING: This is not my letter. The Devil has forged it. You should not have believed that I wrote it. Mother, how could you?

THE KING'S MOTHER: Oh, my son. I am relieved to hear that. I did not carry out your order. Be satisfied that she is still alive. I secretly had a doe killed and took the proof from it.

THE KING: Where is she and my son?

THE KING'S MOTHER: I tied your wife's child onto her back and told her to go out into the wide world, and she promised never to come back here, because you were so angry with her.

THE KING: I will go as far as the sky is blue and will not stop until I have found my dear wife and my child again.

The King immediately takes off and travels – a mime walk.

~ SCENE 12 ~

SET UP: The Forest

THE NARRATOR: Then, The King traveled about for nearly seven years, searching in all the stone cliffs and caves, but he did not find her, and he thought that she had perished. Finally, he came to a great forest, where he discovered a little cottage.

THE OLD MAN: Welcome, Your Majesty. Where do you come from?

THE KING: I've been wandering about for nearly seven years looking for my wife and child, but I can't find them.

THE OLD MAN: Wait here, Your Majesty. I will bring you something to eat and drink.

THE KING: I just want to rest awhile.

The King lies down, covers his face with a handkerchief, and immediately falls asleep.

THE NARRATOR: The Old Man went into the room where The Queen was sitting with her son, now seven years old, whom she called "Sorrowful."

THE OLD MAN: Go outside with your child. Your husband has come.

She goes with her son to where The King is lying. She takes his sword and sticks it to his throat.

THE SON: Mother, who is this man?

THE MAIDEN: He is your father.

The Son takes the handkerchief off The King's face and looks at him.

THE SON: I don't have a father in this world, Mother. You told me that my father is in heaven.

THE MAIDEN: Sorrowful, pick up your father's handkerchief and put it over his face again.

THE SON: Dear Mother, how can I cover my father's face when I have no father on earth?

The King awakens.

THE KING: Who are you?

THE MAIDEN: I am your wife and this is your son.

THE KING: My wife had golden hands.

THE MAIDEN: My natural hands grew back. It was a miracle. I had to have them back to take care of our son on my own.

THE KING: Why are you afraid of me?

THE MAIDEN: I read your letter. You ordered to kill me and our child.

THE KING: Those were not my words. The Devil forged the letter. How could you believe it?

THE MAIDEN: I couldn't believe it, but your mother did. Your own mother believed that you became evil.

THE KING: The Devil deceived even her.

THE SON: Who is The Devil, Father?

THE KING: He is the liar who deceives people and makes them hate each other.

THE MAIDEN: He is gone. I feel that The Devil is gone. I am not afraid anymore.

She lowers the sword and puts it on the ground.

THE KING: Come with me back to the castle.

THE MAIDEN: Take my hands.

He does.

THE MAIDEN: Do you feel them?

THE KING: Yes, I do. They are soft and warm.

He kisses her hands.

THE MAIDEN: Let's go. Come, Son. Take us back to the castle.

They all exit.

~ THE END ~

~ ~ ~

~ Psyche ~

~ A Play ~

by

Christopher Vened

Based on
Hans Christian Andersen's
Story of The Same Title

~ CAST OF CHARACTERS ~

<u>The Narrator:</u> She/he speaks directly to the audience while narrating the story and invoking the action with gestures at the same time.

<u>Lorenzo:</u> A reclusive young artist who seeks perfection in art

<u>Angelo:</u> Lorenzo's outgoing friend who loves life

<u>Adele:</u> A noble girl whose unearthly beauty inspires Lorenzo to sculpt Psyche

<u>Adele's Father:</u> A rich nobleman who commissions Lorenzo to make a marble sculpture of Psyche

<u>Servant in Villa Farnesina:</u> A servant to Adele's family

<u>Francesca:</u> A model for the artists who wants to be sculpted by Lorenzo

<u>Marco:</u> An artist who admires Lorenzo's work

<u>A Group of Young Artists:</u> Free spirited Renaissance artists with whom Lorenzo socializes at the Café Grotto

<u>Viola And Gaia:</u> Two models for the artists with whom Lorenzo dances in Cafe Grotto

<u>Brother Ignatius:</u> A doctor and a priest, who advises Lorenzo to become a Monk

<u>Monks in the Monastery:</u> They initiate Lorenzo to life in the Monastery

<u>Two Gravediggers:</u> They find the sculpture of Psyche in the garden and dig it out two centuries later

<u>Museum Patrons:</u> They admire the sculpture of Psyche, which is displayed in the Museum

~ PLACES ~

The Young Artist's Atelier

A Street in Rome

Villa Farnesina

An Artists' Cafe Grotto in Rome

The Monastery (A Monk's Cell)

The Garden

The Museum

~ TIME ~

Renaissance

~ PROLOGUE ~

SETTING: Rome

AT RISE: The spotlight goes up on THE NARRATOR standing in the middle of the stage.

THE NARRATOR *looks at the imaginary morning star in the sky*: At dawn, the morning star shines brightly. Its rays fall on the white walls of the city as if it wanted to write upon them all the stories it knows: all that it has seen through the thousands of years on earth. Listen! Here is one of its stories: Not long ago - and by "Not long ago" the star means "a few hundred years ago" - its rays followed a young artist who lived in Rome.

~ SCENE 1 ~

SETTING: The Young Artist's Atelier.

THE NARRATOR, *pointing at LORENZO, a young artist, who makes a sculpture in his workshop*: Time has changed the city, but not as rapidly as it changes a human being from infancy to old age. The Church was holy and all-powerful; and art was holy and at its height. In Rome lived the world's greatest painter, Raphael, and that epoch's leading sculptor, Michelangelo. The Pope himself admired these artists and paid visits to their workshops. Yes, artists were esteemed, honored, and even rewarded; but this does not mean that every great talent was recognized. This young artist lived in an old house on a narrow street. He was poor and unknown. But he had friends who knew about his skills and talent.

Lorenzo continues to make a sculpture in his workshop.

ANGELO, Lorenzo's friend, enters.

ANGELO: Good morrow, Lorenzo.

LORENZO: Morrow, Angelo.

ANGELO: What do you have?

LORENZO: What?

ANGELO: What are you working on right now?

LORENZO: Oh, I finished this one yesterday, but today I am not happy with it.

ANGELO: Let me see.

LORENZO: Nothing to see.

ANGELO *looks at the sculpture*: What are you complaining about? It's quite good.

LORENZO: Quite good?

ANGELO, *while admiring the sculpture*: Yes, everything is done well: form and proportions, good counterpoint and balance.

LORENZO: It's just craft, Angelo, technical skill.

ANGELO: Well, not only. It's beautiful. I like it a lot, Lorenzo.

LORENZO: What do you like about it?

ANGELO: Many things.

LORENZO: Can you be more specific?

ANGELO: Well, I like the sensual line of the body and...

LORENZO: I was not after that, the sensual line of the body.

ANGELO: What were you after, Lorenzo?

LORENZO: Don't you see it?

ANGELO: See what?

LORENZO: Yes, it must not be there but only in my head.

ANGELO: What is it, Lorenzo?

LORENZO: It's just another failure, Angelo. It is just that...

Lorenzo takes a mallet and smashes the sculpture into pieces.

ANGELO: What are you doing?

LORENZO: Destroying imperfect creation, Angelo.

ANGELO: Don't do it!

LORENZO: It must be gone! Disappear from the world!

ANGELO: Stop it! Stop it, Lorenzo! You are mad.

LORENZO: It's gone, Angelo! Puff! I smashed it!

ANGELO: Why are you doing it? It is sheer madness. Whatever you create you destroy.

LORENZO: Because I don't like it the next day when I look at it.

ANGELO: Where is the logic of it? You made so many sculptures, and you have nothing to show. You destroy them all.

LORENZO: So?

ANGELO: I could have helped you sell this one. It was really good.

LORENZO: You don't understand, Angelo.

ANGELO: What don't I understand? Tell me, Lorenzo. Tell me.

LORENZO: You see, I don't want to make just another sculpture. There is plenty of mediocre art in Rome. You can find it on every corner of the town.

ANGELO: Your sculptures are not mediocre; you have skill and talent.

LORENZO: It's not enough! Something is missing.

ANGELO: What more do you want?

LORENZO: I want to make a sculpture as good as Michelangelo's or Rafael's paintings. They make masterpieces.

ANGELO: Yes, they do. But you are just a kid. It takes time to become a master.

LORENZO: They made their first masterpieces when

they were sixteen, seventeen years old. You either get it, or you don't.

ANGELO: What is that? What is in their paintings and sculptures that you don't see in your own work?

LORENZO: Infinity.

ANGELO: Infinity?

LORENZO: That something magical or metaphysical that transports you to another dimension, to another world.

ANGELO: Which is?

LORENZO: Spiritual, not from this earthly world.

ANGELO: That's deep.

LORENZO: Yes, it is!

ANGELO: There are plenty of wonderful things to paint in this world.

LORENZO: What are they?

ANGELO: Beauty of natural landscapes, joy of life, beautiful girls, very seductive.

LORENZO: Certainly, they are. I see them too.

ANGELO: So why aren't you satisfied to paint them? All those earthly delights.

LORENZO: I don't know. When I look at Raphael's paintings or Michelangelo's sculptures, all other things become pale in comparison and vanish.

ANGELO: You are a dreamer, Lorenzo, and that is your misfortune, and the cause of it is that you have not lived. You have not tasted life. You ought to take a big healthy swallow from the bottle and enjoy it. Youth and life must be one. Look at the great Master Raphael, honored by the Pope, admired by the world; but he does not say no to either bread or wine.

LORENZO: I heard something about it.

ANGELO: They say he not only eats bread but devours the baker woman as well.

LORENZO: Who is she?

ANGELO: The young and lovely fornarina, Margherita Luti.

LORENZO: No.

ANGELO: Yes.

Angelo starts to leave.

ANGELO: I'll be going!

LORENZO: Okay. It was good to see you, my friend.

ANGELO: We are going to the wine cafe tonight. You know, young artists and models. Would you like to join us for our revelries?

LORENZO: No, not tonight! I think I'll stay and start another sculpture.

ANGELO: All right, if you change your mind, you know where to find us.

LORENZO: I know.

ANGELO: So long, Lorenzo.

LORENZO: See you later, Angelo!

Angelo leaves; Lorenzo starts molding another sculpture in clay.

~ SCENE 2 ~

SETTING: A Street in Rome / Villa Farnesina

THE NARRATOR: One day Lorenzo was passing one of Rome's more splendid palaces. He paused in front of the entrance. Looking through the frescoed archway, he saw a small garden filled with roses. In the center of it there was a fountain, where water splashed into a marble basin. A young girl was there; she was walking - no, floating, for so light was her step - near the fountain. The young artist had never seen anyone so beautiful, so delicate, so dainty, so lovely.

Lorenzo does as the Narrator describes: He walks on the street and stops in front of the entrance of the Villa Farnesina, downstage center. He then looks inside through the archway located above the audience and admires the girl. The Narrator stands behind him like a shadow and looks over his shoulder at what he sees. When the girl disappears from Lorenzo's view, the gleam of astonishment vanishes from his eyes. Then he withdraws and walks back to his workshop.

~ SCENE 3 ~

SETTING: The Young Artist's Atelier

THE NARRATOR: And as he went about his workshop, she remained alive in his mind; and he molded a clay sculpture he named Psyche, which was an image of the young noblewoman.

Lorenzo is molding the imaginary clay Psyche; The Narrator moves around him in unison, echoing and observing Lorenzo at work.

THE NARRATOR: And for the first time he was satisfied with his work. Here at last was something of value: it was the girl.

Lorenzo looks at his work and realizes he got it right this time - a soul is there. He sinks to his knees in gratitude to God, looks up to heaven and then buries his face in his hands and weeps.

THE NARRATOR: He must be in shock, but these tears are of happiness.

Lorenzo regains composure and looks at his sculpture again with utter admiration.

His friends, Angelo, MARCO, and FRANCESCA enter. Lorenzo, transfixed on his work, does not see them.

ANGELO: Lorenzo! Lorenzo, we are here!

LORENZO: Angelo, Francesca, Marco.

FRANCESCA: Good day, Lorenzo.

LORENZO, *still transfixed on his sculpture:* Good day, my friends!

ANGELO: You seem to be in a haze, my friend. Are we welcome here or what?

LORENZO: Yes, please, welcome friends. I have something to show you.

ANGELO: What is it?

LORENZO: Look at it, the sculpture!

FRANCESCA: It's beautiful.

ANGELO: Now I think I know what you were after.

LORENZO: What do you see, Angelo?

ANGELO: I see a living soul captured in clay.

LORENZO: Yes, that is what I was after.

FRANCESCA: What is her name?

LORENZO: Psyche!

FRANCESCA: How suitable.

MARCO: Why?

FRANCESCA: Psyche means soul in Greek.

MARCO: Why is Psyche always portrayed with Eros then?

FRANCESCA: He fell in love with her and made her immortal.

MARCO: I always believed in your talent, Lorenzo, but this sculpture surpasses my highest expectation. It is a masterpiece.

LORENZO: Thank you, Marco.

ANGELO: Were you inspired by the myth of "Eros and Psyche?"

LORENZO: No, Angelo.

ANGELO: What inspired you then. I'm curious.

LORENZO: It was a girl that I saw in the garden of Villa Farnesina.

ANGELO: You were at the Villa Farnesina?

LORENZO: No, I saw her in the garden through the gate. Just a glimpse and then she disappeared. But her image stayed in my mind.

FRANCESCA: Now I am jealous.

ANGELO: Are you fully satisfied this time?

LORENZO: Almost.

ANGELO, *wagging his finger:* Don't destroy it.

LORENZO: No, I will not.

FRANCESCA: I can sit for you, sometimes, if you like.

LORENZO: You are too expensive for me, Francesca. I am a poor artist.

FRANCESCA: For you, I will do it for free, Lorenzo. I want to be immortalized by you like this girl from the Villa Farnesina.

LORENZO: I will think about it, Francesca.

They leave.

~ SCENE 4 ~

SETTING: The Young Artist's Atelier

THE NARRATOR: One day a party of wealthy Romans came to the humble street where the young artist lived. They had come to see his work; but the star does not tell us how they had happened to hear about it. Poor young man! Or should we say too happy young man? There before him, in his own workshop, stood the young noblewoman.

A party of wealthy ROMANS, five or six of them, enter Lorenzo's workshop. Among them are ADELE, the noble girl Lorenzo saw at the Villa Farnesina, and ADELE'S FATHER, a rich nobleman. They admire the sculpture of Psyche.

ADELE'S FATHER: But it is you, Adele!

Adele looks at the sculpture of Psyche with utter admiration and smiles. In that moment The Narrator makes a magical gesture and freezes the picture. All characters become motionless except Lorenzo, who looks at Adele's smile with adoration and imagines how he would reproduce that smile in clay or marble. Lorenzo acts out his imagination.

THE NARRATOR: The girl smiled! And the artist could see that smile reproduced in his sculpture, or her glance, which ennobled and crushed him.

The Narrator makes another magical gesture and brings the picture back to realistic motion.

ADELE'S FATHER: You must make that figure in marble.

LORENZO: I will.

ADELE: That would be lovely.

ADELE'S FATHER: When it is finished, I shall buy it.

LORENZO: Thank you.

ADELE'S FATHER: Let me know when you are done working on it.

LORENZO: I will.

ADELE'S FATHER: Farewell for now.

LORENZO: Farewell, noble guests.

~ SCENE 5 ~

SETTING: The Young Artist's Atelier

THE NARRATOR: These words brought life to the dead clay, to the heavy marble, and to the young artist. A new era began in the workshop: a time of joy and laughter. The morning star watched the work progress.

Lorenzo makes a sculpture of Psyche anew in marble, while The Narrator moves around him, as an invisible observer, narrating the process to the audience at the same time. The Narrator must be fully involved.

THE NARRATOR: The marble block was raised and tools made ready. The first rough work was done. Measurements were made and marked in the marble and large pieces of it chopped away. Soon the young artist had to use all his craftsmanship and skill to give shape to the stone. The beautiful figure of Psyche appeared. She was so light, she seemed about to take flight. She danced, she smiled, and in her smile was reflected the innocence of the young artist.

Lorenzo makes finishing touches and then becomes elated with his work.

LORENZO *talks to the sculpture of Psyche*: Now I know what life is, it is love! It is to be able to appreciate loveliness and to delight in beauty.

LORENZO *sinks to his knees in front of his sculpture of Psyche; he is in awe*: My Psyche... You must be mine forever.

LORENZO *stands up*: I love you.

Angelo enters.

ANGELO: Lorenzo!

LORENZO, *pointing at the sculpture*: Angelo, come and see my Psyche.

ANGELO: She is perfect.

LORENZO: Yes, she is.

ANGELO: It is even better in marble than in clay. The smooth whiteness of marble makes it divine. And that archaic smile you added, it is so alluring.

LORENZO: It is not archaic; it is her smile.

ANGELO: Who's smile?

LORENZO: Adele's smile.

ANGELO: The girl from the Villa Farnesina?

LORENZO: Yes.

ANGELO: Are you in love with her?

LORENZO: Yes, I am madly in love with her. And I am going to see her today.

ANGELO: Be careful, Lorenzo, she is a noblewoman.

LORENZO: I am noble too.

ANGELO: Since when?

LORENZO: I am an artist. I have been given God's grace; it makes me noble.

ANGELO: You made a masterpiece, Lorenzo! Soon the whole world will admire your Psyche. That is your reward.

LORENZO: My Psyche! Yes, she must be mine. My work shall be immortal.

~ SCENE 6 ~

SETTING: *A Street in Rome / Villa Farnesina*

THE NARRATOR: He went to the palace to report that the marble statue had been finished.

Lorenzo walks to the palace. He stops downstage center and looks above the audience. Then he turns and through this symbolic transition finds himself inside the palace. A SERVANT in livery approaches him.

SERVANT: Who are you, goodman, and what is your errand?

LORENZO: I am an artist, and I made a sculpture for the noble family of this house. His Lordship asked me to come when the sculpture was ready.

SERVANT: Follow me, sir.

They go to the hall and meet Adele's Father.

ADELE'S FATHER, *enthusiastically*: Lorenzo, a young master artist, you are welcome in my home.

LORENZO: Thank you, Signore.

ADELE'S FATHER: Is my sculpture ready?

LORENZO: Yes, it is ready.

ADELE'S FATHER: It's impressive that you made it so quickly.

LORENZO: I was inspired, Signore.

ADELE'S FATHER: That's wonderful. My daughter was already asking about it. She is so impatient, as if she cannot understand that it takes time to make a sculpture in marble.

LORENZO: Yes, it does.

ADELE'S FATHER: Well, I am curious to see it too. I will send someone to your workshop to pick it up. And then we will finalize the transaction.

LORENZO: Thank you, Signore! It was my honor to make a sculpture for you and your daughter.

ADELE'S FATHER: Lorenzo, before you go, I want you to talk with the young Signorina, Adele, my daughter. I think she will be delighted to hear about this sculpture that looks so much like her, from you, the artist, the creator of it.

LORENZO: I would be delighted to tell your daughter all about it.

~ SCENE 7 ~

SETTING: Villa Farnesina

THE NARRATOR: When the interview was over, Lorenzo went to see the nobleman's daughter. A servant accompanied him through beautiful banquet halls and galleries, all filled with sculptures, paintings, and frescoes, until, finally, they came to the chamber of the young girl.

While The Narrator is talking, Lorenzo follows the servant, captivated with the rooms and the art. They arrive at Adele's chamber, and Lorenzo suddenly finds himself in front of the young girl.

SERVANT: Signorina, your father wondered if you would like to talk with this artist.

ADELE: Lorenzo, a young talented artist. I certainly would like to talk with you, sir.

LORENZO, *dumbfounded*: I would, I would...

ADELE: What?

LORENZO: I am so delighted to see you again, Signorina. Your beauty is even more than I imagined.

ADELE: What is the news that you bring me, sir?

LORENZO: I've finished the sculpture... it is ready.

ADELE: Does it look like me?

LORENZO: It does.

ADELE: Why do you call it Psyche?

LORENZO: I captured your soul in it.

ADELE: How do you do it? How can you capture a

living soul of a person in marble? I mean, my soul. You say you captured my soul.

LORENZO: I love you, Adele! It was a work of love. You are so beautiful and noble. I adore you. You are my muse. I worship you.

Lorenzo goes on his knees, grabs Adele's hand and kisses it. Adele at first appears surprised, then insulted, and finally proud and full of disdain, as if her hand has mistakenly touched the damp, clammy skin of a toad.

ADELE: Madman!

LORENZO: I am sorry.

ADELE: Leave me alone!

LORENZO: Please, don't be offended, Signorina. I will do anything you want. You are my ideal and I am your slave. Forgive my outburst, forgive me.

ADELE: Go away!

LORENZO: Oh, no!

ADELE: Help!

The servants come.

SERVANT: Signorina, what's going on?

ADELE: Take this madman away from me.

LORENZO: Please, don't do it to me, Signorina. I am begging you for forgiveness. I meant no harm. Please, listen to my supplication. I simply admire you with my whole heart.

ADELE: How dare you, you ugly toad, how dare you talk to a noblewoman like that?

Lorenzo is flabbergasted and stands there frozen, transformed to stone.

ADELE: What are you waiting for?

ADELE, *to the servants*: Take him away!

LORENZO: Signorina...

ADELE: Leave me alone!

LORENZO: Signorina!

ADELE: Go away!

The servants assist Lorenzo out of the Palace.

Lorenzo walks as The Narrator describes the action.

THE NARRATOR: He made his way out of the palace as lifelessly as an object sinks into the sea. Once on the street, he walked like a sleepwalker; but when he reached his workshop he awoke in rage and pain.

~ SCENE 8 ~

SETTING: The Young Artist's Atelier

Lorenzo convulses in rage and pain. He goes on his knees, tears his hair from his head, and then bangs his head on the floor. He cannot take it anymore. He scratches his face. Angelo enters the workshop, unnoticed to Lorenzo, and observes his friend in distress.

Lorenzo grabs his mallet and lifts it; he is about to destroy the marble statue of Psyche, but Angelo grabs his arm and stops him.

ANGELO: What were you about to do? Have you gone mad?

Lorenzo charges at the sculpture again. Angelo grabs him and they wrestle. Angelo is stronger. Lorenzo gives up and collapses listlessly on the ground.

ANGELO, *kindly*: What has happened? Pull yourself together and tell me.

Angelo's questions are answered by silence.

ANGELO: This is about the girl from Villa Farnesina, isn't it?

LORENZO: Yes.

ANGELO: Do you want to tell me what happened?

LORENZO: No, I don't.

ANGELO: Why not?

LORENZO: It was like a bad dream, a nightmare.

ANGELO: Your blood will grow thick and stop flowing from all your dreaming! I don't want dreams but reality. Admit that you are a man. If you live only for your ideals, then life will break you! Drink some wine, get a little drunk, and you will sleep better. Let a beautiful girl be your physician. The girls of the Campagna are as lovely as the princess in the marble castle. Both are daughters of Eve, and in paradise you would not be able to see the difference between them. Be a man and come with me. Let Angelo be your guide, your angel of life.

LORENZO: Okay, Angelo, I will.

ANGELO: Come with me.

LORENZO: Where?

ANGELO: To the Grotto Cafe.

Lorenzo and Angelo go out.

THE NARRATOR: Angelo had come at the right time. A fire was burning in the young artist's blood; his soul seemed to have changed, he wanted to tear himself away from the life he had led, from all his old habits.

~ SCENE 9 ~

SETTING: *The Artist's Cafe Grotto*

THE NARRATOR: On the outskirts of Rome was a little restaurant that was a favorite meeting place for young artists. It was built in the ruins of an ancient bath and was located in a deep vault that resembled a grotto. Some tables stood outside, under the lemon and laurel trees.

During the description, the actors bring tables and chairs and arrange the cafe space, while getting in character of the patrons. They are YOUNG ARTISTS. Lorenzo and Angelo enter the Cafe. Their friends greet them with shouts of joy.

YOUNG ARTISTS (*ad-lib*): Angelo! Angelo? Come over here. Wow, Lorenzo! Welcome, friend, to our company. Welcome!

ANGELO: Marco, Federico, Francesca, Pietro, Paolo, look whom I brought here: our good friend, Lorenzo.

MARCO: Good e'en, Lorenzo.

LORENZO: Good e'en, Marco, Pietro, Francesca,...

FRANCESCA: Look who is here!? Lorenzo, at last you are with us. Come sit next to me.

Lorenzo and Angelo sit down between their friends.

ANGELO: Bring us some wine.

People are pouring and drinking wine.

YOUNG ARTISTS (*ad-lib*): Drink, Lorenzo, drink! Salute. Have some more. Cheers!

LORENZO: Wait a minute. Slow down a bit. I didn't eat anything yet. Can I get something to eat?

YOUNG ARTISTS (*ad-lib*): He wants something to eat. Lorenzo wants something to eat. Ha, ha, ha. Bring him something to eat. To drink? No, to eat. He wants to eat first; he wants to eat. Ha, ha, ha.

LORENZO: Why is everybody laughing, Angelo?

ANGELO: Lorenzo, we eat little, or not at all, but drink a lot, for wine makes you cheerful.

YOUNG ARTISTS: Let's drink! Let's drink!

They drink. They sing and someone begins to play music. It is a saltarello, an Italian lovely jumping dance, and they start to dance.

Two Roman girls, VIOLA and GAIA, who earn their living as models for the artists, join in the lively dance.

ANGELO, *pointing to Viola and Gaia*: Look at these two bacchantes, Lorenzo.

LORENZO: Who are they?

ANGELO: Viola and Gaia, our models, we paint and sculpt them.

LORENZO: Lovely girls.

ANGELO: Look at the way they dance.

LORENZO: As if they were on fire.

ANGELO: They have hot blood, Lorenzo, they have passion for life. Would you like to join them in a dance?

LORENZO: Oh, no, I've never danced in my life!

ANGELO: Viola, Gaia...

Angelo joins them.

VIOLA/GAIA: Angelo, Angelo. Who is your serious friend?

ANGELO, *calling*: Lorenzo, Lorenzo, come over here and meet the girls. This is Viola, this is Gaia.

Lorenzo timidly waves to them. The girls dance around him.

VIOLA/GAIA: Come and dance with us, Lorenzo.

LORENZO: No, thank you, I don't know how to dance.

ANGELO: Let yourself go, let the currents that are flowing all around you and within yourself carry you.

VIOLA/GAIA: Oh, come on, dance!

One of the girls grabs Lorenzo by the hand and pulls him to the floor. He yields, and all of them dance. The girls work him out; he loosens up and becomes liberated.

THE NARRATOR: How hot it was that day, even after the sun set. Blood was afire, air was afire, and there was fire in every glance. The air seemed filled with gold and roses; that was the substance of life, gold and roses.

Time has passed and Lorenzo is drunk and jubilant now. He dances with one of the girls; they whirl wildly, he loses his balance and falls on the floor. Angelo picks him up.

ANGELO: Are you all right?

LORENZO: Yes, I am all right, Angelo.

As he says it, he reels and almost falls again.

ANGELO: How are you feeling, Lorenzo?

LORENZO: Never before have I felt so well and happy. You are right. All of you are right! I have been a fool, a dreamer. Man belongs to the world of reality, not to the world of the imagination. I want more wine!

ANGELO: Slow down, Lorenzo. Have you eaten anything?

LORENZO: We eat little but drink a lot...

He grabs a bottle of wine from the nearby table and drinks it with abundance.

LORENZO: For wine makes you cheerful - ha, ha, ha.

Lorenzo becomes crazy out of his mind: drinking, grabbing girls, talking nonsense. He tries to kiss Viola and Gaia. They push him away.

ANGELO: Let's take him home, he is drunk. Come on, Lorenzo.

Angelo holds Lorenzo up by his shoulders. Others assist him.

YOUNG ARTISTS (*ad-lib*): Let's go! Everybody. Where are we going? To Paulo's atelier.

ANGELO: Let's drop Lorenzo home on the way first.

YOUNG ARTISTS: Let's go.

They walk on the street. Angelo, with Viola and Gaia's help, drags Lorenzo. They reel and stagger. Lorenzo pushes

Angelo away and stands in the middle of the street.

LORENZO, *exalted:* Apollo! Jupiter! To your heaven do I want to ascend. Now, at this moment, for the first time, the flower of life is blooming in my heart.

VIOLA/GAIA, *playfully:* What flower? I want a flower, Lorenzo. Give me a flower.

LORENZO: I give you a rose, Viola.

GAIA: What kind of flower will you give me, Lorenzo?

LORENZO: I give you a carnation.

VIOLA/GAIA: You are sweet.

The girls and Angelo take drunken Lorenzo and drag him onward.

~ SCENE 10 ~

SETTING: The Young Artist's Atelier

Angelo, Viola, Gaia, and Lorenzo arrive at his atelier. He is out of it. Angelo drops Lorenzo on the bed. He mumbles unintelligibly in a drunken stupor.

Viola and Gaia admire the (imaginary) sculpture of Psyche. They become playful and strike poses of Psyche on their own.

LORENZO: You smell like roses, Viola. And you, carnations, Gaia. You are a rose, and you are a carnation. Blooming, everything is blooming.

Lorenzo becomes uneasy about Viola and Gaia striking poses of Psyche. We see them from his drunken point of view now. It becomes hallucinatory.

THE NARRATOR: Yes, it bloomed, bent its head, and withered. A strange, horrible smell of corruption blended itself with the odor of roses, it lamed his mind and blinded his sight. The fireworks of sensuality were over, and darkness came.

Lorenzo becomes nauseous.

LORENZO *mumbles*: It's stuffy here. I need some fresh air.

ANGELO: What are you saying?

LORENZO: Roses, carnations, blooming.

VIOLA: He's wasted.

ANGELO: Yes, he is.

GAIA: Let's go, Angelo. Let's go to Paulo's atelier. Everybody is there.

ANGELO: Are you going to be all right, Lorenzo?

LORENZO, *spasmodically:* Shame, shame, shame!

ANGELO: Hey, what's wrong, my friend?

Lorenzo does not answer and falls asleep.

GAIA: Let him sleep it off. He'll be fine.

VIOLA: Let's go, Angelo.

GAIA: Angelo let's go!

ANGELO: All right.

He covers Lorenzo with a blanket, and they go.

THE NARRATOR: His thoughts became unclear, and he fell asleep.

~ SCENE 11 ~

SETTING: The Young Artist's Atelier

THE NARRATOR: At dawn he awoke. What had happened? Was it all a dream: the visit to the restaurant, the night with the girls of the Campagna? ... No, it was real; and now he knew a reality that he had never known before.

Adele enters. The Narrator takes her by the hand and leads her to the pedestal of (imaginary Psyche. Adele stands on the pedestal and assumes the pose of Psyche.

Lorenzo wakes up, struggles with his thoughts, feels horrible, dirty, sullied. He feels painfully ashamed of debasing himself with life last night. He feels guilty of betraying Psyche, so to speak, his purity and innocence. He gets up, crawls to the sculpture of Psyche and curls in a fetus position at her feet.

LORENZO: Forgive me, forgive me, forgive me! I am so sorry, so sorry. Oh, what a poor wretch I am. I will never do it again. I promise.

He kisses her feet.

PSYCHE/ADELE: Wretch! Leave me alone. Go away!

Lorenzo stands up and backs off. He goes back to bed and suffers. The morning light brightens and shines upon the marble Psyche/Adele. He looks at her and trembles when he sees the divine innocence of the sculpture.

He approaches the sculpture; Adele/Psyche looks at him.

LORENZO: Why are you looking at me like that?

First, he turns away and covers his face in his hands. But then, he stands up, approaches the sculpture of Psyche and touches it. He caresses the sculpture the way a sculptor would do when making final touches, echoing its shape.

LORENZO: It's perfect!

PSYCHE/ADELE: Leave me alone. Go away!

He takes his hands away as if afraid to sully it. He backs off.

LORENZO *whispers:* I cannot take it anymore.

He makes a final attempt to touch the sculpture again but can't. It's over. He lost the touch.

LORENZO, *sad, distressed:* I can't, I can't.

He runs back to bed and hides under the covers. In the meantime, The Narrator takes Adele by her hand and leads her off the pedestal. Then she lets her go off stage.

Lorenzo gets up. He mimes throwing a cloth over the (imaginary) sculpture and wraps it up with a rope. He does it with care and sadness. Then he lifts the heavy marble sculpture and carries it out into the garden, where there is an abandoned well. Lorenzo throws the marble Psyche into it. Then he fills the hole with earth, and spreads branches and nettles over the burial place. He does it all with a grave manner. We shall get the impression that he performs a funeral rite of departing from his lover, so to speak, his art.

PSYCHE/ADELE (*voice over*): Leave me alone! Go away!

He covers his ears not to hear it; and goes back to his workshop.

~ SCENE 12 ~

SETTING: The Young Artist's Atelier

Lorenzo sits motionless on the ground.

THE NARRATOR: Days passed and weeks. The nights were the longest. Silently, motionlessly, turned inward, into himself, he sat through the long day. He knew nothing about what was happening outside in the world, and no one knew what took place within him, in his soul. Everyone who saw him agreed that he was dying.

BROTHER IGNATIUS arrives.

THE NARRATOR: From the nearby monastery Brother Ignatius arrived. He was both a friend and a physician.

BROTHER IGNATIUS: Praise be to God!

LORENZO: Brother Ignatius, what brings you here?

BROTHER IGNATIUS: People say you are not well, Lorenzo. You look pale and weak. Are you sick?

LORENZO *whispers:* I don't know.

BROTHER IGNATIUS: Let me check your temperature.

LORENZO: Please, do.

Brother Ignatius put his hand on Lorenzo's forehead.

BROTHER IGNATIUS: You are feverish. Do you have chills?

LORENZO: Yes.

Brother Ignatius examines him: checking his pulse, listening to his lungs, checking his eyes and tongue.

BROTHER IGNATIUS: You are not sick, Lorenzo! Yet you are dying. What is wrong?

LORENZO: I don't know.

BROTHER IGNATIUS: Tell me the truth. Open your heart, Lorenzo. I am your friend and a priest. I came to comfort you with religion.

LORENZO: My heart is broken, Brother Ignatius. I feel ashamed and humiliated with life. I don't want any more disappointments.

BROTHER IGNATIUS: I thought that you found fulfillment in art. You were a very talented sculptor. Why don't you sculpt anymore?

LORENZO: I can't.

BROTHER IGNATIUS: Why?

LORENZO: I don't have an inspiration. I've lost it.

BROTHER IGNATIUS: How so?

LORENZO: It was an error. Do you understand?

BROTHER IGNATIUS: No, I don't.

LORENZO: My art was a sin, my cardinal sin.

BROTHER IGNATIUS: Go on. Confess it.

LORENZO: Art was only an enchantress who with her magic gave me vain dreams of earthly glory. I fell for it. But it was all false.

BROTHER IGNATIUS: How?

LORENZO: She can make us all false to ourselves, false to our friends, false to God. The snake was ever whispering: "Taste and you shall be a god." So I did. I thought, "I have power of creation as God has." But it was deceptive. It was only illusion of art. I fell for it. I was deceived by the devil. I was proud. Not anymore.

BROTHER IGNATIUS: Are you still tormented with it?

LORENZO: Yes, I am. And it incapacitates me. I will never sculpt again.

BROTHER IGNATIUS: What are you going to do?

LORENZO: I don't know how to do anything else but art. Sculpting was my only passion. There is nothing I can do, nothing I want in this world. I don't see the way.

BROTHER IGNATIUS: You don't fit to this world, Lorenzo. You don't have earthly desires. Don't force it but come with me and join the monastery. Sacrifice yourself to God and become a servant of the Church. Will you?

LORENZO: Yes, I will.

THE NARRATOR: And his words fell like the rays of the sun on the moist, fermenting earth. A mist rose, and in a mist can be seen strange shapes and pictures. From these "islands" floating above him, the young artist saw himself looking down at all mankind.

Brother Ignatius gives Lorenzo a hand and helps him to stand up. Then the stage transitions to the next scene that takes place in the monastery.

~ SCENE 13 ~

SETTING: The Monk's Cell

MONKS appear and transform the space. They ritualistically greet Lorenzo and dress him in a monk's frock, while in his hands is placed a rosary.

THE NARRATOR: How kindly, how happily his new brothers greeted him, and how like a festival on a high holy day it was when he took his vows. He felt that now, at last, he had found the road to truth and peace. In the Church, God's light shone in all its glory; in the tranquility of the monk's cell his soul would know eternity.

Lorenzo kneels and prays silently with a rosary in his hands.

THE NARRATOR: At sunset, he stood at the open window of his cell and looked out over the ancient city with its crumbled temples and gigantic but dead Colosseum.

Lorenzo stands at the open window.

THE NARRATOR: He felt himself to be more alive and to feel more deeply than he ever had before. Everything melted into one, everything spoke of peace and beauty: a fairy tale, everything was a dream!

Lorenzo kneels in his cell and prays.

THE NARRATOR: Yes, the world was a dream. Dreams can reign for hours and can be recaptured for hours, but life in a monastery is made up of years: many years, long years. Unclean, evil thoughts come from inside yourself, he learned.

Lorenzo becomes tormented by his thoughts.

THE NARRATOR: What were these strange flames that seemed to set his body on fire? Where did the evil come from, which he wanted no part of, yet always seemed to be present within him?

Lorenzo flogs himself with a whip.

THE NARRATOR: He punished his body, but the evil did not come from the surface but from deep within him.

~ SCENE 14 ~

SETTING: A Street in Rome

THE NARRATOR: One day, many years later, he met his friend Angelo, who recognized him immediately.

Lorenzo and Angelo meet on the street.

ANGELO: My friend!

LORENZO: Angelo!

ANGELO: Lorenzo, are you happy now?

LORENZO: Your words sound like an accusation. What do you have against me, Angelo?

ANGELO: You have sinned by throwing away the gift God gave you.

LORENZO: I am serving God.

ANGELO: What have you won? What have you sought and what have you gained? Is your life not a life of dreams? Have you not created religion out of your own head, as all monks do? What if it is only a dream? Only imagination? Only beautiful thoughts?

LORENZO: Satan, leave me alone.

ANGELO: Lorenzo, you are my friend.

LORENZO: I don't want to see and speak with you ever again. Go away!

Lorenzo flees from his friend.

~ SCENE 15 ~

SETTING: The Monk's Cell

LORENZO, *talks with God/the Audience*: That was the Devil... My personal Devil. I recognize him. O my God, have mercy. Once I gave him a finger and he grabbed my whole hand....

No, that is not true. The evil is within me. And it is within Angelo. Yet to him it is no burden. He holds his head high and seems to prosper. And I... I search for happiness in religion! But what if it is only a consolation? What if there is no heaven but only vain dreams: an illusion that disappears as the beautiful pink color of the sunset when you come close to it?

Eternity, you are a great ocean of endless stillness. You fill us with curiosity and foreboding; you beckon and call; but if we step out upon your quiet waters we disappear, die, cease to exist. This is fraud! Deceit!

Lorenzo feels penetrating chill in his body. He feels that his death comes near. He panics and wants to flee from the monastery. He struggles to stand up but is not able to keep his balance and collapses.

LORENZO: Is it the end?.......... Leave me alone!

He fights with an invisible death.

LORENZO: Go away!

He composes himself again and sits still in a meditative position.

LORENZO: There is nothing within me, and there is nothing outside me. My life has been wasted.

THE NARRATOR: And this thought grew, like snow sliding down the mountainside, until it was an avalanche that crushed him.

Lorenzo begins sobbing spasmodically, falls on the ground and convulses. He is tormented. He identifies with the crucifixion and performs stigmatization. Then freezes in the position as if he were crucified on the cross.

LORENZO: No one do I dare tell about this worm within my heart. This secret is my prisoner; if I told it, I would be its captive.

THE NARRATOR: Faith and doubt wrestled within him. The deeper he looked into his soul, the darker it seemed to him.

LORENZO: O Master! Master! Have pity on me and give me faith. I threw Your gift away. Your purpose I ignored.

I did not have the strength! You gave me the skill and talent but not the strength!

Pain seizes him in his heart.

LORENZO: Immortality is in my heart! The Psyche - leave me alone! Go away! Why can you not be buried like the Psyche I once created? That one part of my life, let it remain buried in the grave, never to be resurrected.

He is exhausted.

THE NARRATOR: The star of dawn shone brightly; someday even that star will cease to be. Only the human soul is immortal.

LORENZO: The Psyche within my heart will never die. Will it be conscious forever? Can that which is beyond understanding happen? Yes! Yes! That which is incomprehensible is my own soul! O God, O Master, it is You and Your whole world that are beyond understanding and let it remain so: a wonder of power and glory and love.

THE NARRATOR: His eyes brightened and then they grew glazed.

The sound of the church bells is heard.

THE NARRATOR: The ringing of the church bells was the last sound he heard in this world; the man was dead.

~ SCENE 16 ~

THE NARRATOR: Centuries later, the morning star shone as before, as brightly as it had for thousands of years. Yet what she had seen then and now has much changed. Where there once had been a narrow street and an old house in which lived a young artist there now stood a convent. That morning a young nun had died, and a grave was being dug in the cloister's garden.

Two GRAVEDIGGERS dig a grave, miming it.

GRAVEDIGGER ONE: My shovel is getting stuck on stone.

GRAVEDIGGER TWO: What is it?

GRAVEDIGGER ONE: Something brilliantly white.

GRAVEDIGGER TWO: Lift the earth carefully, it's marble.

GRAVEDIGGER ONE: I see a shoulder and a woman's head.

GRAVEDIGGER TWO: It's a sculpture.

GRAVEDIGGER ONE: Let's pull it out!

They pull the sculpture of Psyche out and bring it to an upright position.

GRAVEDIGGER TWO: Wow!

GRAVEDIGGER ONE: It's beautiful.

THE NARRATOR: The sculpture of Psyche was unearthed while a grave was being dug for a nun. And it was taken to a museum for a display.

~ SCENE 17 ~

SETTING: The Museum

The transition from graveyard to a museum takes place in a few fluid moves. The two Gravediggers withdraw while Adele enters. The Narrator takes Adele by her hand and leads her to the pedestal center stage. Adele stands on the pedestal as a sculpture, assuming the pose of Psyche. The museum's PATRONS enter, surround the sculpture and admire it.

MUSEUM PATRONS (*ad-lib*): Wow, oh, ah ... It's beautiful. Sublime. Outstanding. Wow, it is a masterpiece.

THE NARRATOR: Everyone agreed that it was beautiful.

PATRON ONE: But whose work is it?

PATRON TWO: Who was the master who created it?

The Narrator makes a magical gesture and freezes the museum's Patrons into a tableau.

THE NARRATOR: No one knew but the star of dawn, who knew of his earthly struggle, his trial, his weaknesses, his humanity. But all that was dead, had disappeared, turned to dust. But his gain, his profit from his struggle, and the glory that proved the godliness within him, his Psyche, will never die. It will live beyond the name of its creator. His spark still shines here on earth and is admired, appreciated, and loved.

The Narrator unfreezes the museum's Patrons from the tableau, and they become animated again.

MUSEUM PATRONS *(ad-lib)*: Wow, oh, ah... It's beautiful. Sublime. Outstanding. Wow, it is a masterpiece.

THE NARRATOR: It is his soul that he carved in marble that they admire - His own immortal Psyche.

~ THE END ~

~ ~ ~

~ ABOUT THE AUTHOR ~

Christopher Vened is originally from Poland, where he had an illustrious career as an actor in the internationally renowned theatre company, the Wroclaw Pantomime Theatre of Henryk Tomaszewski. When martial law was declared in Poland at the end of 1981, Christopher defected to the West for political reasons. First, he stayed in West Berlin, where he worked in Transformtheater and founded his own company, Impuls. Then, in 1984, he permanently moved to the USA, where he rebuilt his career teaching acting, choreographing, directing, and writing plays. He wrote the acting book, *In Character: An Actor's Workbook for Character Development,* which is published by Heinemann Drama since 2000. His writing credits include a one-man show *Human Identity;* a play *Infidel;* and *A Theatrical Memoir: An Interview with Myself.* Recently, he wrote *The Theater Manifesto of an Old Man*, where he talks about his own philosophy of theatre. He leans towards the theater of meaning, and believes that in modern, postmodern culture, meaning has been relativized, or distorted, or lost, and needs to be restored or rediscovered.

His most delightful project was the theater production of *Three Stories*, which consists of three plays based on classical fairy tales *The Emperor's New Clothes, The Maiden Without Hands,* and *Psyche*. He was commissioned to write these plays by the Acting Conservatory of OCSA, where he also directed the plays in the school's Studio Theatre, in the fall of 2019.

www.ingramcontent.com/pod-product-compliance
Lightning Source LLC
Chambersburg PA
CBHW050412030726
47503CB00006B/2148